MY TRUE COMPANION

It is 1921. Social pariah Millie Woodridge is obliged to obtain employment as a companion for ageing actress, Mrs Oakengate, when her father is unjustly executed on charges of espionage. During a weekend house party Millie meets handsome adventurer, James Haxby, and is soon drawn into the dark, but thrilling world of espionage. Unsure who to trust, Millie joins James in tracking down a callous murderer and uncovering the truth about her father.

SALLY QUILFORD

---◆---

MY TRUE COMPANION

Complete and Unabridged

LINFORD
Leicester

First published in Great Britain in 2010

First Linford Edition
published 2012

British Library CIP Data

Quilford, Sally.
My true companion. - -
(Linford romance library)
1. Love stories.
2. Large type books.
I. Title II. Series
823.9′2–dc23

ISBN 978–1–4448–0966–4

Published by
F. A. Thorpe (Publishing)
Anstey, Leicestershire

Set by Words & Graphics Ltd.
Anstey, Leicestershire
Printed and bound in Great Britain by
T. J. International Ltd., Padstow, Cornwall

This book is printed on acid-free paper

1

England 1921

Mrs Oakengate navigated the green Bullnose Morris Oxford up the driveway of Fazeby Hall. 'Didn't I tell you it was spectacular, Millicent?' she said. 'The Fazebys have owned this manor house for five hundred years. They're very old money . . . not titled but one can't have everything . . . and very dear friends of mine.'

High above them, a flag bearing the Fazeby family coat of arms flew from one of the corner towers of the solid Tudor manor house. Spreading out behind and on either side was a vast estate. 'Sadly they lost many of their servants in the war, so Cynthia has warned us we may have to dress ourselves this weekend. It is impossible to get good servants nowadays. Even those who survived look down their noses when offered honest work as a footman. In my day people accepted their lot. The rich man in his castle, the poor man at his gate. Tell a man he's a hero and suddenly he forgets his station in life.'

Millie Woodbridge, who was used to dressing herself, said, 'You were right, Fazeby Hall is magnificent, Mrs Oakengate.' Aged twenty-four, and dressed in a demure grey pinafore over a white blouse, she had a fresh, pale face and a glossy chestnut bob covered with a plain cloche hat.

Mrs Oakengate's hat, over an Eton crop, sported a flamboyant bow, which more than once had threatened to cover her eyes as she drove. 'Ah,' she said, being helped out of the car by a footman, 'here's Cynthia Fazeby.'

A slender, woman, aged about forty, with an ageless beauty and natural style stood on the steps of Fazeby Hall. She wore the latest fashion with the air of a woman who did not really care what she wore, and yet somehow managed to look stunning. She walked down to them and held out her hand. 'Victoria, darling, how wonderful to see you. And this must be your charming new companion.'

'Yes, this is Millicent Woodbridge,' said Mrs Oakengate. Cynthia held out her hand to Millie. 'Her father was the spy, Richard Woodbridge. They hanged him a few months ago, if you remember.'

Millie caught her breath. She had not expected her father's alleged crime to be spoken of so openly, and was not prepared for how to deal with it. 'Millie's mother, Amelia was my friend, in my early days as an actress.' Mrs Oakengate carried on regardless. 'Poor Millie here doesn't have her mother's beauty, but she's a sweet enough child.'

Cynthia squeezed Millie's hand and said gently, 'I am very sorry for your loss, child. I knew your mother and father many years ago, before my marriage. I continue to believe your father was a good man.'

'Thank you,' Millie said, deeply moved. 'That's very kind of you. I believe he was a good man too.'

'Sadly the jury didn't think so, dear,' said Mrs Oakengate. 'Now, Millicent, would you stay here and make sure the servants get the suitcases to the correct rooms?' she said as two elderly servants appeared.

It was not in Millie's job description to deal with the luggage but she agreed, guessing that Mrs Oakengate and Cynthia Fazeby wished to speak together in private.

'So,' said Mrs Oakengate, putting her arm through Cynthia's, 'who is coming this weekend? A lot of very interesting people, I hope.' They walked up the steps to the front door, leaving Millie alone, but Cynthia looked back and gave her a regretful but encouraging smile.

'Would you believe James Haxby?' she said to Mrs Oakengate. 'We fully expect him to come crashing through the window.'

'How exciting! I hear he's very handsome. And that name. Haxby. They say it's to do with Vikings. And by all accounts he is a bit of a Viking.'

'I don't think he has to ravage and pillage, dear. Women are apparently queuing up to offer him favours and he's rich enough not to need to steal from others.'

'Maybe I'll offer him my favours,' said Mrs Oakengate, as she disappeared inside.

Millie strained to hear what was said, but they'd already gone out of earshot. Everyone knew the famous adventurer James Haxby. Millie's father had often followed his exploits in the papers, reading out the particularly exciting parts to her over the breakfast table. Haxby had walked the Amazon basin, taken food with African tribes, and more than once had become involved in some local trouble that he'd helped solve with his charm and intelligence. She doubted he would notice her presence, but it was exciting to know that she would be meeting him. She only wished her father could meet him.

With that melancholy thought, she supervised the carrying of the luggage upstairs, feeling embarrassed to be telling the servants their business. It wasn't the done thing to get in their way, especially when they were well able to do the job without her help. They seemed to sense her discomfort, treating her with the same kindness that their mistress had shown.

She had been given the room next to Mrs Oakengate. It was small, but very pretty, the wallpaper decorated with forget-me-nots. The centre was dominated by a big comfortable bed. She sat on it for a moment, wishing that she had a little more time to herself. She was used to being alone, and liked it, but since taking up the post of paid companion to Mrs Oakengate, time alone was a precious commodity.

Not that Millie only wanted to sit still and think. It was just that she felt there must be something more interesting to do in life than go for dress fittings, dining out and calling upon friends, all of whom only ever talked about the same things.

She missed her father dreadfully. She had helped him with his experiments into new types of flying machine, which were faster and safer. Experiments that the British government believed he had shared with the enemy. The evidence, the prosecutor said, was overwhelming. Pictures had been taken of Richard Woodbridge, at a grouse shoot, meeting with a known agent of the enemy. The same agent had been found dead, clutching a blueprint, which had been signed by Millie's father. The fact that her father denied all knowledge of the man, and had only met him socially at an event attended by several dozen other people, including several members of parliament, was not believed.

Sighing, Millie tried and failed to push all thoughts of the past aside. Before his death, she promised him that she would survive to see his name cleared. How she could do that, she did not know. She had written letters to the Home Secretary, but she knew that was not enough. Somewhere there must be proof that he had not betrayed his country. If only she knew where to look for that proof. Unfortunately for Millie, her father's pension from the Civil Service had been stopped as soon as they found him guilty. She had no income of her own. She lived off their savings whilst he was in prison, and then had to give up their rented house after his execution because she could no longer afford to live there. A kindly neighbour had let her board with them, taking, Millie was sure, far less than they could have got by advertising the room. She had applied for secretarial posts with other inventors, but her name was blackened because of her father. No one would take her on. She was left with no choice but to accept Mrs Oakengate's offer.

She silently chastised herself for being so ungrateful. If not for Mrs

Oakengate, she would have nowhere to live.

Realising she had to go back downstairs and face everyone, she took a deep breath and went out onto the landing. A few doors down, she could hear voices coming from one of the bedrooms. One of them was Cynthia Fazeby's. The other was a man, whom Millie took to be Cynthia's husband, Henry Fazeby.

'She should never have brought that girl to Fazeby Hall,' Cynthia Fazeby was saying.

'That's the trouble with Victoria,' said Henry, 'she never does think how awkward it is for others when she produces pieces from her collection. Remember the daughter of the acid bath murderer who was her secretary for a while?'

'Yes,' said Cynthia. 'More's the pity.'

Millie hated to be thought of as an unwelcome visitor. She crept down the stairs, hoping her presence on the landing had not been noticed. She wished she could run out of the front door and never come back.

Millie felt no animosity towards the Fazebys. She sympathised with their discomfort. That would not make the weekend any easier for her. She vowed to make herself as invisible as possible.

2

The butler showed Millie to the drawing room, where she was relieved to see a familiar face.

'Uncle Alex,' she said, as her godfather stepped forward to greet her. Alexander Markham had been her father's closest friend. Aged sixty, he was still very handsome, and drew admiring glances from Mrs Oakengate, who sat draped across the window seat. The rest of the room was furnished in a regency style, with plush sofas and comfortable chairs.

'Millie, my dear girl,' Alex said, kissing her cheek. 'I had no idea you were going to be here.'

'I'm with Mrs Oakengate,' said Millie, gesturing towards her employer.

'So she's been telling me,' said Alex Markham, with an amused twinkle in his eyes. 'I'm sorry I haven't seen you

11

for a while. I've been in Argentina, you know, working for the government.'

'I understand,' said Millie. In truth she'd been disappointed that Uncle Alex had been so far away. But he had written to give his condolences, which was more than any of her surviving relatives had done. 'There was nothing much you could have done.'

Alex squeezed her hand. 'I miss him.'

'So do I.' They were both silent for a few moments.

'Now then,' said Alex. 'In the absence of our delightful hostess, let me introduce you to some of the other guests, my dear. This is Mr and Mrs Parker-Trent. Mr and Mrs Parker-Trent, allow me to introduce my god-daughter, Millicent Woodbridge.'

A couple, who had been watching with obvious interest, stepped forward to greet Millie. Arthur Parker-Trent was a man in his fifties, balding and with bright red cheeks. Millie had heard of him as a well-known industrialist, who was at that time, taking on the unions. Mrs Parker-Trent could not have been more than Millie's age, with dyed blonde hair and bright red lipstick. She had the look of someone who had worked in a dress shop, and spoke in an affected way.

'How nice to meet you, Miss Woodbridge. Arthur and I were only just saying the other day what a terrible tragedy your father's death was.'

'You said that, I didn't,' said Mr Parker-Trent. 'A man who betrays his country deserves to die.'

'He didn't,' said Millie, with quiet dignity.

'I'm sure he didn't,' said Mrs Parker-Trent.'

'Ignore my wife,' said Mr Parker-Trent. 'She has a knack of saying just what people want her to say, which is how she fooled me into marrying her. Whereas I'm an honest man. You can't put a price on honesty, I always say, regardless of hurt or offence.'

'You are such a kidder,' said Mrs Parker-Trent, colouring. 'Don't listen to him, Miss Woodridge. He doesn't mean half of what he says.'

'I do, you don't,' said Parker-Trent, darkly.

Millie felt sorry for Mrs Parker-Trent. What her husband said may well be true, but Millie sensed that under all the make-up, Mrs Parker-Trent felt as unsure of herself as Millie did.

'And,' said Alex, 'we also have Mrs Barbara Conrad. She's a novelist, Millie, so I'm sure you'll have a lot to talk about.'

Mrs Conrad lacked Mrs Parker-Trent's glamour and Cynthia Fazeby's beauty, reminding Millie of a hockey teacher from school, yet she had a kind, thoughtful face that Millie warmed to immediately. She seemed rather shy and awkward. 'How do you do, Miss Woodbridge?'

'How do you do?' said Millie, holding out her hand. 'I'm afraid I haven't yet read any of your books.'

'You're not alone in that,' said Mrs Conrad, smiling ruefully. 'And I'm very sorry for your loss.' There was a shrewdness in her eyes, despite her apparent shyness, that suggested a sharp and insightful mind.

'Barbara was just telling us that her next book is due out soon,' said Victoria Oakengate from the window. 'You must tell Millicent all about it, Barbara. She likes reading. Speaking for myself, I find it a bore. Real people are so much more interesting. Whilst I don't wish to discourage you, my dear, I hardly think people will take to an Austrian detective.'

'Argentinean,' said Mrs Conrad. She and Millie exchanged amused glances, which made them immediate friends.

'I should like to read it,' said Millie, not just being polite. She adored murder mysteries, and had often read Sir Arthur Conan Doyle's novels aloud to her father.

'I have a few copies with me. Not that I'm in the habit of carrying them and forcing them on people.' Mrs Conrad laughed awkwardly. 'My publisher insisted I sign some for posterity whilst I'm here. I'll be happy to let you borrow one,' Mrs Conrad said.

'That's very kind, thank you.'

'I believe we are just waiting for the arrival of Count Chlomsky and Mr Haxby to make our party complete,' said Alex.

'Chlomsky . . . now where have I heard that name?' asked Mrs Oaken-gate.

'Count Victor Chlomsky is an inventor of weapons,' said Alex Markham. 'He's a Prussian, but switched to our side during the Great War. Now he's a citizen of one of those little European states that no one can pronounce.'

'Oh yes,' said Mrs Parker-Trent. 'I read about him in the papers. He's very brave. A true hero.'

'Ironic, isn't it?' said Mrs Conrad, in her quiet way, 'that a spy who switches to our side is hailed a hero, whereas someone who is only believed to have worked for the other side . . . '

Mrs Parker-Trent looked at Mrs Conrad blankly, but Millie understood

16

the inference and blessed Mrs Conrad for it.

At that moment the doorbell rang, and a few minutes later, a grand looking man with a magnificent beard entered the room. He reminded Millie of King Edward, but with a foreign flare lacking in the old king.

'Count Chlomsky, how good to see you again,' said Alex Markham, almost falling into the role of host. He introduced everyone else to the Count. Mrs Parker-Trent went so far as to give a little curtsey.

The assembled guests made small talk, until their hosts arrived to take the role from Alex Markham.

'I do apologise,' said Cynthia Fazeby. 'We've been the most dreadful hosts. Henry had to take a telephone call from London, and the line was dreadful. It seems Mr Haxby won't be arriving till much later. He insisted we all go into dinner without him.

Dinner was a polite though rather strained affair. Millie had changed into

17

the only evening dress she owned, a gown of fine grey muslin, which her father used to say made her look like a shadow. Her heavy fringe curved over her large dark grey eyes. She finished the look with grey satin slippers, hoping that she could indeed melt into the shadows.

Mrs Oakengate and Mrs Parker-Trent dressed as though for dinner with the King. Mrs Oakengate wore deep red silk, and Mrs Parker-Trent competed in blue velvet. Mrs Conrad wore a simple blue gown, and Cynthia Fazeby wore a dress of antique lace, with tiny pearls around the neckline.

Cynthia and Henry Fazeby were old hands at putting people at their ease, and the urbane Alex Markham was at home anywhere he went. Despite their efforts, there was an underlying tension that Millie could not put her finger on. Chlomsky in particular seemed to be under some stress, drinking heavily, and becoming redder in the face as the night wore on.

She wondered if it were because of her presence, and as the dessert of lighter-than-air lemon sorbet was served, prayed for an excuse to escape.

Mrs Conrad was watchful, taking an interest in everyone. She also made an effort to draw Millie into the conversation, though if Millie were honest, she would rather keep out of it. She had spent very little time in the outside world over the previous couple of years and was not familiar with any of the people or politics the diners discussed. For two years, her life had revolved around her father's trial. Everything else faded in significance. As such, she found herself very ignorant of current affairs.

'Those damned socialists,' Arthur Parker-Trent was saying. 'Encouraging workers to form unions. I won't have it in my workplace, I tell you, despite the workers trying to force it on me. If we're not careful we shall all be murdered in our beds and taken to the guillotine.'

'The guillotine would be rather redundant if one had already been murdered,' said Henry Fazeby, to general laughter. 'Still, your lovely wife would make a most charming Marie Antoinette.'

'It is often said I look as though I have blue blood,' said Hortense. 'And dear papa . . . '

'Papa was a milkman,' said Arthur Parker-Trent.

'He was an eccentric rich man,' Hortense said, her cheeks flaming. 'We had our own dairy farm.'

'Dash it all, Hortense, you come from a grimy little street in Derbyshire. Not far from here in fact,' Arthur retorted.

'The Peak District is very beautiful,' Millie said, feeling sorry for the young woman.

'Yes, it's wonderful,' said Hortense, her voice losing its affected tone. 'The Heights of Abraham has one of the best views in the country, especially in autumn, when the leaves turn russet. I used to go there as a girl.' Her eyes took on a faraway look, making her face look genuinely pretty. 'I'd climb Masson Hill in the evenings, just to watch the sunset.'

'I should like to see it,' said Millie.

'So would I now that you've described it so beautifully, Hortense,' said Mrs Conrad. Arthur Parker-Trent harrumphed into his glass of wine. 'Perhaps we could travel there this weekend.'

'I should hate it,' said Victoria Oakengate. 'The countryside is a bore. Not in your lovely home, of course, Cynthia. But I despise trees.'

'We shall try to keep them off the itinerary,' said Henry Fazeby, wryly. Millie got the impression that he would much rather be locked up in the library with his books than hosting a dinner party.

When the butler brought the port, the women retired to the drawing room. 'I know it's an old-fashioned custom to leave the men to their port,' said Cynthia Fazeby, as she led them through to the drawing room, 'but I prefer to chat without the men — womens' conversation is far more interesting.'

'So,' said Mrs Oakengate when the women were alone. They sat back in comfortable chairs, drinking coffee. 'Tell me about Chlomsky. Is he rich?'

'Very,' said Cynthia, her eyes glowing mischievously. 'His family were something important in Prussia. Are you thinking of husband number two?'

'Oh, always darling. Though I would much rather Alexander Markham. Millicent, you must tell me all about your godfather.'

Barbara Conrad, sitting in the corner browsing through a magazine, raised her eyebrow, then winked at Millie.

'He's a very kind, intelligent man,' said Millie. 'When I was growing up, he was like a second father to me. We — I haven't seen him for a while.'

'He's a great diplomat,' said Cynthia. 'Henry tells me that many a time Alexander has got the country out of trouble abroad. Not quite in the same way as James Haxby but . . . '

'Now, tell me about Haxby,' said Mrs Oakengate, her mind already having moved on. 'He's quite the adventurer, I hear.'

'Oh yes,' said Cynthia. She related what was known of Haxby's adventures, all of which seemed incongruous when sitting in a civilised drawing room in the middle of England. Mrs Parker-Trent listened with rapt attention. Much of it Millie already knew from the papers, but there were other hints at dangers not made public. Then the talk moved on to more mundane things. Dresses, hats, and who was seeing whom, and the local area. It was decided that they would visit the Heights of Abraham the following morning and take tea in one of the cafés in Matlock.

'I wonder . . . ' said Millie after a while, 'if I might excuse myself.' She looked to Mrs Oakengate for permission.

'My dear child,' said Mrs Oakengate, 'you'll have people thinking I keep you as a slave. You may retire anytime you wish.'

That wasn't strictly true, and there had been several nights when Mrs Oakengate had insisted on Millie sitting up into the early hours listening to her employer reminisce. Millie supposed it was loneliness.

'Millie, if you would like to read my book,' said Mrs Conrad, 'come to my room in half an hour and fetch it.'

'That's very kind, Mrs Conrad, thank you.'

'Please, call me Barbara.'

* * *

Fazeby Hall began to settle down for the night, as Millie made her way to Barbara Conrad's room on the opposite wing of the building. She had waited to ensure Mrs Oakengate was settled for the night, to prevent being called in for a 'chat' which would have meant another night of not getting to bed until three in the morning.

'Come on in, child,' said Barbara. It seemed an odd thing for her to say, since she was only a few years older than Millie. 'The maid has left us two cups of cocoa and some biscuits, so I hope you will stay a while and talk.'

Millie smiled her gratitude. Barbara beckoned to a comfortable chair near the window. 'I always hate these country house weekends,' she said. 'But it is expected of one's class to attend them occasionally. It's always worse when one is alone.'

'Is your husband busy this weekend?' asked Millie, just to make conversation. A dark cloud passed over Barbara's face. She sat on the edge of the bed, nursing her cup of cocoa.

'Yes, he's working. Tell me about Mrs Oakengate. How did you find yourself working for her?'

'She and my mother were on the stage together, before I was born.'

'Your mother is dead, isn't she?'

'Yes, she died when I was little. I don't remember much about her. Just vague impressions. Sometimes I'll hear a song or smell a particular perfume and it reminds me of her . . . ' Millie stopped. 'I'm sorry. You're not interested in all that.'

'Yes, I am, Millie. Did your father never remarry?'

'No, though there was a lady who visited for a while. But Papa was married to his work. So it was just the two of us. I used to help him. I hoped that I'd be able to get a job working with another inventor, but sadly my name does not instil them with confidence.'

'So now you're stuck with Oakengate.'

'Oh, she's very kind to me,' said Millie. 'If not for her I might have to work in a factory.'

'She's not a kind woman,' said Barbara Conrad, emphatically. 'You're not the first trophy she's paraded in public. Victoria Oakengate collects people. I'll say one thing for her, she's not a snob. She's probably a better person than me in that sense. She doesn't mind if people are flat broke, as long as they either come from the right family or come from a family so notorious that she can dine out on their infamy. She should never have brought you here.'

'I realise my presence must be embarrassing . . . '

'It's not you, Millie,' said Barbara. 'Victoria should never have thrust you into the spotlight like this. Especially with Count Chlomsky attending.'

'What has he got to do with anything?'

'You don't know? No, I suppose much was kept out of the court case. My husband hears things however, and it's believed that Count Chlomsky was one of the men to whom your father gave secrets.'

'Then why was he not also charged with spying?' asked Millie, horrified.

'Because by the time they found out,

he had become a citizen of a friendly country and was made a diplomat. They have immunity, as you probably know.' Barbara put her cup on the bedside table. 'I shouldn't have said anything. It's just that you looked so uncomfortable tonight and I sensed you felt unwelcome. The fact is Cynthia Fazeby is more than happy to have you here. It's Count Chlomsky's presence that's the bugbear.'

Millie decided not to tell Barbara about Cynthia and Henry Fazeby's discussion. 'So why was he invited?'

'He more or less invited himself, I believe. He and Parker-Trent have business dealings. As the Foreign Office want to keep an eye on him, they asked Cynthia and Henry to play along.'

'He's not a nice man.'

'Who, Chlomsky? No I suppose he isn't.'

'No, sorry, I meant Mr Parker-Trent.' Millie had not made up her mind about Count Chlomsky, not having had much opportunity to speak to him. The fact he might have known her father played on her mind. As Millie had no doubts at all about her father's innocence, she now wondered exactly what part Chlomsky might have had to play in his downfall.

'I agree. He's very unkind to that silly wife of his and she's a harmless soul really,' said Barbara. 'It's a very common way to behave. But he's a very common man. With far more common beginnings than his wife, by all accounts. Now he has his eye on a knighthood and other accolades. In fact, it was a surprise to everyone when he married Hortense. Everyone expected him to marry above himself, to help him get a leg up into high society.' Barbara smiled, a mischievous gleam in her eyes. 'I hope we shall be friends, Millie. If you need to talk to anyone whilst we're here, please consider my door always open.'

Once again, Millie was moved. Cynthia Fazeby and Barbara had shown her the first genuine kindness she had known since her father was arrested.

On some occasions, when leaving the court, she had been abused on the street. Others were polite, but distant. Even the few friends they had known, including girls of Millie's own age, had drifted away, not wanting to be associated with the family. The kind neighbours who gave Millie a home did it out of pity for her and not because of Millie's father, whom they thought must be guilty if the court deemed it so.

It was strange how that changed after her father's execution. Then people began to see Millie as a tragic victim and, despite her father's alleged crime, saw him as some sort of anti-hero to be both admired, due to his assumed forage into espionage, and yet despised at the same time. Barbara Conrad showed Millie no pity, only kindness and a sense that they were equals.

The two women chatted for a little while longer, before Millie wished Barbara goodnight, clutching a copy of the good lady's novel in her hand.

As she walked along the corridor, the

door to one of the bedrooms opened to reveal Hortense Parker-Trent. Her face was clear of make up, and she was dressed in a simple nightgown, looking younger, fresher and prettier, apart from dark lines circling her eyes.

'Miss Woodridge,' Hortense whispered, looking up and down the corridor, 'I need to speak to you.'

'Hortense . . . ' It was Mr Parker-Trent, calling his wife in a querulous voice. 'Come back to bed this instant.'

'Tomorrow,' said Hortense. 'When we go to the Heights of Abraham. I'll speak to you then. It's really important.'

Millie nodded in agreement, before Hortense quickly slammed the door. Millie could hear Mr Parker-Trent's harsh voice from inside, and Hortense's softer tones, placating him. Realising she was in danger of eavesdropping on intimate marital discussions, Millie continued towards her room.

At first, Millie only saw long shadows, cast along the hallway by the faint electric lamps. Then a man appeared at the top of the stairs. He was tall and muscular, with rugged features, his hair thick and dark, devoid of the oils and potions many men used. It was also slightly longer than the norm, his fringe falling over his eyes, which were hazel brown. He looked like a man only just in touch with civilisation, like an animal that had only recently been tamed and might easily revert to a savage state at any moment.

'I heard that Fazeby Hall had a ghost called The Grey Lady, but I hardly expected to meet her on my first night,' he said in deep tones, his piercing gaze searching Millie's face. There was an old roof supporting beam across the ceiling, on which he rested his hand, towering above her, making her feel even smaller and more insignificant than usual. 'Or that she would be so lovely . . . and strangely sad.'

'I am not a ghost, sir,' she said, trying to sound braver than she felt. 'I'm a guest. Millicent Woodridge.' She held out her hand.

'Richard's girl?' he said, his eyes widening. 'Dear God, why are you here?' He took her hand, but did not let go as Millie expected him to.

Her cheeks felt hot. 'I am companion to Mrs Oakengate. But if you object to my being here . . . ' She pulled her hand away.

'No, certainly not. Forgive me,' he said, his voice softening. 'I just wasn't expecting to see you. This makes things more interesting. Very interesting indeed. Are you brave, Millicent?'

'Not very,' she admitted.

'I don't believe you. Your father was brave, right to the end. You have something of him in you, the way you meet my gaze head on. I like that.'

It was news to Millie. What she really wanted to do was look down, run, to get as far away from this disconcerting man as she could. 'You are Mr Haxby, I presume,' she said.

'That's me. Adventurer and all round good egg.'

'Are you, sir?'

'Stop calling me sir. I'm not your schoolmaster — this is nineteen-twenty-one — my name is James. Or Jim when you get to know me better.' He said the latter with a degree of intimacy that made Millie blush even more.

'I doubt we will become that well acquainted,' she said, smiling shyly.

'What a pity,' he said, looking at her with those deep hazel eyes. 'I shall just have to be haunted by you for the rest of my life.'

'It may be safer that way,' said Millie. For whom she didn't know. 'Goodnight, Mr Haxby.' She slipped past him and ran to the safety of her room, where despite her best efforts to forget, she spent the rest of the night remembering his piercing eyes.

3

Victoria Oakengate cried off from visiting The Heights of Abraham, preferring to remain in the comfort of Fazeby Hall. Henry Fazeby announced that he had too much to do on the estate. James Haxby was nowhere to be seen at breakfast, and his batman informed Cynthia that Mr Haxby had slept in but would join them later.

The party travelling in several cars to Matlock on the bright spring morning consisted of Millie, Cynthia Fazeby, Count Chlomsky, Alex Markham, Mr and Mrs Parker-Trent and Barbara Conrad. Millie travelled with her god-father.

Millie would never have admitted it publicly but it felt good for her to get out from under the shadow of Mrs Oakengate. She felt light-hearted for the first time in a long time.

'It is good to see you, Millie,' said Alex, who had deliberately engineered things so that he and Millie had a car to themselves. 'Especially now we're rid of that dreadful woman. Really, child, whatever possessed you to become her companion?'

'The need to eat and have a roof over my head,' said Millie, quietly. 'You know that Papa's pension was stopped. I spent all our savings on his legal defence and renting a room.'

'I will ask around Whitehall,' said Alex. 'There's bound to be a job you can do there.'

'I can't imagine they'll take me on, under the circumstances. I had thought of attending secretarial school. Unfortunately that costs money, and I'd need somewhere to live.'

'Why didn't you say, dear girl? I could have . . . '

'Thank you, Uncle Alex, but I can't take your charity.' Millie stuck her chin out proudly.

'How many Christmas and birthday

presents have I bought you over the years? How many times have I taken you out to lunch?'

'I can't remember.'

'That's because I've hardly ever done it. I'm the worst godfather in the world. I owe you rather a lot of gifts and lunches. I'll give you the money you need to go to secretarial school and enough for living expenses.'

'I'll have to think about it,' she said. 'It's just . . . well people might think there was something improper going on, now that Papa isn't here.'

Alex looked shocked. 'My dear girl,' he said, 'I do hope you don't think that I was suggesting . . . '

'No, no, of course not.' Millie reached out and touched his arm. 'Only that, well, you know how people talk.'

'Of course,' said Alex, keeping his eyes firmly on the road ahead. 'We could get over all that if you were to marry me.'

'What?' Millie was shocked. Her god-father's proposal had come from nowhere, and even though they weren't related in

37

any sense of the world, it somehow felt wrong. 'I . . . Uncle Alex . . . '

'That was rather silly of me, wasn't it?' he said, laughing, as though the idea really meant nothing to him. But Millie sensed it did, and that the proposal had come from the heart. It was both flattering and disturbing. 'Let's pretend I never said it. But if you ever find yourself in dire straits, I hope you will at least consider my offer, rather than starve to death.'

'Thank you,' said Millie, gazing out of the window, trying to quell the unease in her heart.

They could have taken the tram up Masson Hill, but as it was a beautiful morning, they decided a stroll would be more pleasant. Halfway up, Millie sensed that more than one of the party regretted turning down the tram. Count Chlomsky and Arthur Parker-Trent, neither in the peak of physical fitness, struggled with the climb. Hortense strode up the hill as if it were all flat, whilst Cynthia, Barbara and

Millie tried hard to keep up with her. Alex Markham, though not struggling as much as Chlomsky and Parker-Trent, brought up the rear. When Millie looked back, he was deep in thought.

'Is your godfather well this morning, Millie?' asked Barbara Conrad. Cynthia and Hortense had gone on a little further.

'Yes, he's . . . I think I might have offended him,' said Millie.

'I find that hard to believe? What did you do?'

Millie hesitated, feeling she did not really know Barbara well enough to tell all her secrets. Yet the lady had shown nothing but kindness to her. 'He asked me to marry him, and I refused,' said Millie.

Barbara looked taken aback. 'Well . . . yes, it's rather a surprise isn't it? I don't mean it's a surprise that anyone would want to marry you, dear child. Only . . . well . . . ' She floundered and stared ahead.

'I know. He's much older than I am,

and I almost think of him as a second father,' said Millie. 'So I was rather disturbed by the proposal. Not that I think anything untoward. I'm sure Uncle Alex only means to try and care for me, now that Papa is gone, and it was his clumsy way of doing that. He's not in love with me, nor I with him.'

'Yes, I'm sure that's it,' said Barbara. She turned her head to Millie and smiled. 'But do be careful, Millie. With that lovely face, you'll be a target for many men in the future.'

'I seriously doubt that,' Millie said, blushing. Before her father was arrested a few young men had called to their house, and one of them had even taken Millie out to see a moving picture. He disappeared from their lives the moment her father was sent to trial, and the last Millie heard he had married an American heiress and emigrated to New York.

'Don't listen to Mrs Oakengate,' Barbara said. 'You're a very pretty girl. Quite beautiful even.' There was some reserve in the way she said it, her lips tightening at the corners. Millie supposed she was just being kind.

The ascent was worth it for the magnificent views over the Peak District, and down to the pretty spa town beneath them. Finally assembled together, the group stood together, looking out and catching their breath.

The Heights of Abraham were named after the battlefield in Quebec where General Wolfe lost his life fighting against the French in seventeen-fifty-nine. The peaceful view seemed at odds with the heat of war.

'It is not as beautiful as Prussia,' said Count Chlomsky. 'But sometimes the British countryside has its own peculiar charm.'

'No better place on earth,' said Alex Markham.

'That's true,' said Barbara Conrad. 'The beauty of the British countryside can't be beaten, I don't care what you say, Count Chlomsky.'

'Ah, Madam, we all love our own country best.'

'And yet you left your country,' Millie said unassumingly, but then watched as she waited to see what the Count's reaction would be.

'That is true, young lady, I did. But loving one's country and approving of one's leaders is a very different thing.'

'It was for love that General Wolfe died in Canada,' said Barbara.

'That and to get a British foothold in Canada,' said the Count. For a man who had changed sides during the war, he sounded less than flattering about the country he had aided.

'I can see why you love it here,' Millie said to Hortense.

'Yes, it's my favourite place,' said Hortense. She seemed subdued. Millie didn't like to think of Mr Parker-Trent being cruel to his wife, but his tone the night before suggested he was more than capable of brutality.

'You said you wanted to speak to me,' said Millie. 'Last night?'

'She's changed her mind,' said Mr Parker-Trent, cutting in before Hortense could speak. 'I've told her not to poke her nose into matters that don't concern her.'

'It was probably nothing,' said Hortense, in a voice that suggested fear and resignation all in one.

'Well, isn't this a wonderful sight?' a voice said behind them. 'A tribute to a man who promised to leave Canada to famine and desolation, and yet accused the enemy of not behaving in a gentleman-like manner.' It was James Haxby and he looked to be completely unfazed by the climb up the hill. He was also looking directly at Millie. 'Ah, I see the ghost of Fazeby Hall has escaped her bonds. Good morning, Millicent.'

'Good morning, Mr Haxby,' said Millie.

'Oh,' said Hortense. 'You're the adventurer.' Her sullen face changed, her ruby red lips turning up at the corners. 'I'm Hortense Parker-Trent.' She held out her hand.

'And I am her husband,' said Mr

Parker-Trent brusquely, casting a furious glance at his wife.

'You have my deepest sympathy, Mrs Parker-Trent,' said Haxby, ignoring Mr Parker-Trent's obvious fury. 'Cynthia, how are you?'

Cynthia Fazeby stepped forward and kissed him on the cheek. 'I'm very well, you naughty boy. Let me introduce you to the rest of the party.'

'It's alright, I know Mr Markham. How are you Markham? And Mrs Conrad. I believe we met in Argentina not long ago.'

'Yes, I was there with my husband,' said Barbara. She said it as if Haxby had challenged her, yet his statement had sounded innocent enough.

'I'm afraid he and I didn't get the chance to meet,' Haxby said. 'Away on business, wasn't he?'

'Yes, that's correct.'

'Count Chlomsky.' Haxby held out his hand but something in his eyes when he looked at the Count perplexed Millie. Was it open hostility or simply

44

wariness? Haxby didn't seem the type to hide his emotions.

Millie was used to people who behaved with great politeness, regardless of their true feelings. In Haxby she saw a man who had no intentions of holding anything back. It both impressed and unnerved her. Even more so when he stood next to her, looking out over the Peak District. 'I must admit the name suits the place,' he said. 'The view is almost biblical in its outlook, taking in all of God's beauty.'

'We were just saying there were few finer places,' said Barbara Conrad

'I have seen finer,' said Haxby, 'but none that stir the heart quite so well as the Peak District.'

'Goodness, Jim, you could have waited for me.' Mrs Oakengate gasped from somewhere below them. She was struggling up the hill in inappropriate footwear. It irked Millie, for reasons she did not quite understand, that Mrs Oakengate was already calling Haxby by a name that he himself had said was

45

saved for his more intimate friends. 'He refused to use the tram, so I had no choice but to walk up too. Whatever happened to helping a lady?'

'You need a gentleman for that,' said Haxby. 'And I'm no gentleman. Besides, women over thirty have the vote now by all accounts — you can climb your own hills.'

'He's such a tease,' gasped Mrs Oakengate, finally reaching the top. 'He talks like a socialist at times.'

'Do you not believe that women should have the vote, Mr Haxby?' Millie asked brazenly.

'Only those who know what to do with it.' He cast a glance at Hortense and Mrs Oakengate.

'Do all men know what to do with their votes?' asked Millie.

'Millicent! I will not have a companion of mine speaking in such reactionary terms,' said Mrs Oakengate. 'Do forgive her, Jim. You are aware, I'm sure that Millicent has suffered a loss recently. Her father was . . . '

'Richard Woodridge. Yes, I know. I'm sure that if any of us dared to forget, you would soon remind us, Mrs Oakengate,' said Haxby, quietly. 'After all, what other claim to fame have you nowadays?' That latter was said in even quieter tones, and Millie suspected that if Mrs Oakengate heard it, she pretended not to.

'Now we've climbed that blessed hill, shall we go back down?' Mrs Oakengate asked. 'I saw a tea room at the bottom. Had Jim not told me the hill was not as steep as it looked, I'd have stayed there.'

Haxby looked directly at Millie with amusement in his eyes. She hid her laughter in a discreet cough.

As Mrs Oakengate decreed, the group began to descend the hill, heading towards the tea room.

Later Millie would try hard to remember the order in which everyone went down the hill, but Haxby's presence by her side for the entire journey downhill cleared her mind of all else. There had been several people climbing the hill, but she had not taken much notice of them either. She was too intent on looking ahead, so that she would not catch his eye. At one point she nearly slipped; and felt Haxby's warm hand on her waist, preventing her from going flying.

'Are you all right?' Haxby asked, showing more gallantry than he had shown her employer.

'I may not have the vote yet, but I can get up and down a hill,' she said.

'I'm sure you can, Millicent,' he said. 'Or do your friends call you Millie?'

'Most people, except Mrs Oakengate, call me Millie.'

'Come along, Millie, Haxby,' said Alex Markham, overtaking them, with Barbara Conrad not far behind. 'Race you to the tea rooms!'

'Where is Hortense?' asked Mr Parker-Trent when they were all seated and tea had been served. The table was laden with fruit scones, Victoria sponge and homemade biscuits. Despite the hearty breakfast served at Fazeby Hall only a couple of hours earlier, everyone tucked in, the climb having given them all a good appetite.

A young girl served them, clearly overwhelmed by the sudden influx of customers out of season.

'I don't suppose she'll be bringing that hot water anytime soon,' said Parker-Trent, shaking the empty teapot.

'Give the girl a chance,' Haxby said, 'she's only just run in with the extra scones you ordered.'

'I was saying to Millicent yesterday that you can't get good servants nowadays,' Mrs Oakengate said.

'I know,' said Haxby. 'It's disgusting, people thinking they don't want to clean up all the mess left by the idle rich.'

'You're being provocative again, Jim,' said Cynthia Fazeby. She addressed him in motherly tones, despite her only being about five years older than him.

'Really?' Haxby's eyes gleamed and there was a noticeable change in his tone when he talked to Cynthia, which suggested to Millie that he liked their hostess. 'I thought I was just being facetious. Provocative is much more interesting.'

'You are a provocative man,' Mrs Oakengate said, smiling coquettishly. 'I don't believe you mean half of what you say.'

'I promise you, Mrs Oakengate that I always mean everything I say.'

'Where in damnation is Hortense?' said Mr Parker-Trent, looking at his watch. Millie looked around and for the first time realised Parker-Trent's young wife was missing.

'I thought she came down Masson Hill with you,' said Barbara Conrad.

'She decided to stay up there a while longer,' said Parker-Trent. 'Damn her to hell, she's never where she should be.'

'I could go and find her,' said Millie.

'No, I'll go,' said Parker-Trent. 'I want to speak to her alone.'

'He's an odious man,' said Haxby

when Parker-Trent had left the tea room. He had taken the seat next to her in the café, she guessed, or perhaps she hoped, because it was as far away from Mrs Oakengate as possible. 'Treats that little wife of his very badly, no doubt.'

'It isn't for us to delve into the private affairs of a married couple,' said Alex Markham, stiffly.

'Quite,' said Haxby, 'meanwhile women are mistreated and have nowhere to go when they need help.'

'I thought you believed we could climb our own hills,' said Millie. Really she wanted to ask Uncle Alex whether he truly believed it was all right to ignore abuse, even in a marriage. His remark seemed at odds with the man she knew. She wondered if he were a little jealous because of Haxby sitting with her. That might account for his reserve.

'Whilst men have more physical power than women there are some hills that can never be climbed,' said Haxby,

51

grimly. 'Not until society treats those men with the disdain they deserve. It says something bad about this country that a man can be hanged for stealing to feed his family, yet we allow those who mistreat their wives and children to go free under the cloak of marital privilege.'

'What a reactionary you are, Jim,' said Mrs Oakengate, her eyes shining with excitement. She clearly found him very attractive, despite the fact that he treated her with disdain. 'It's a wonder they don't hang you for some of the things you say.'

'No, they only hang innocent men in this country,' said Haxby. Millie gasped, and bit her lip, desperate to stop herself from crying. Unable to quell her emotions, she stood up and went outside.

Haxby immediately followed her out. 'That was very cruel of me, Millie. Please accept my apology,' he said.

'What? To call my father innocent?' said Millie. 'On the contrary, it was a very kind thing to say.'

'I'm not a kind man, though. You know that, don't you, Millie?'

'Yes, I think I know that.'

'But I normally reserve my unkind comments for those I believe deserve them. Like the ghastly Oakengate, and Parker-Trent.'

'And Chlomsky?'

'Chlomsky? I don't know what he deserves. Yet.'

Millie was prevented from asking what 'yet' meant by sudden shouting and yelling. People were running down Masson Hill, followed by a stricken looking Parker-Trent.

'Get a rescue team!' a man shouted, running to them. 'And a doctor.'

'What is it?' asked Haxby. 'What's happened?'

'It's this gentleman's wife.' He pointed to Parker-Trent.

'Is she hurt?' asked Millie, feeling her legs weaken as a sense of doom overtook her. She struggled to remain composed. She did not want to be one of those women who fainted at the first sign of any problems.

'She's fallen off the cliff,' Parker-Trent said, his cheeks pink with exertion. 'Landed on a ledge. We think her back is broken.'

4

Millie watched as the men walked up Masson Hill, ready to meet the rescue team. 'Let the men do what they need to do,' Mrs Oakengate told Millie sternly, as the women waited for the car outside the café. 'When this weekend is over, Millicent, I think you and I need to talk. I am not best pleased with the way you are pushing yourself forward with Mr Haxby. I don't mean to be unkind . . . '

'Then don't be, Victoria,' said Cynthia Fazeby, quietly but firmly. 'There is enough distress today, with poor Hortense in such danger. Let's not add to it with trivial concerns.'

'I . . . very well, Cynthia, as we are your guests, I shall hold my tongue.' Mrs Oakengate glowered at Millie.

'We need tea,' Cynthia said to the butler when they arrived back at the hall. 'Lots of it.'

Henry Fazeby came out from his study. 'Is it true, what I've heard? Mrs Parker-Trent is injured?'

Cynthia nodded. 'Then I think this calls for something more than tea,' said Henry. 'Brandy all around I think.' He turned to the butler, who nodded. 'You girls look stricken.'

They retired to the drawing room, where Mrs Oakengate knocked her brandy back and immediately asked for another. Millie sipped hers, not quite liking the taste, but too polite to refuse Henry's ministrations. He was very attentive to them all, in the old-fashioned way of treating women like birds with broken wings.

Despite all that, Millie liked him and his wife very much, and felt sorry that she had caused them so much embarrassment by being at Fazeby Hall. Not that any of that mattered with Hortense Parker-Trent in such danger.

It mystified Millie how someone so used to the Heights could end up in difficulties. Surely Hortense would know not to walk too near the edge. Or perhaps . . . Millie tried to dismiss all of her dreadful thoughts as they came into her head. Hortense might have seemed unhappy, but that would be no reason to take her own life.

The men returned two hours later. Alex Markham entered the drawing room, and stood with his back to the fire, as if ready to make a speech he would rather leave to someone else.

'Mrs Parker-Trent?' said Cynthia, frowning.

He shook his head. 'We did all we could. Young Haxby climbed down to her, but she was already close to death. They took her to the hospital, but we're told she was dead on arrival.'

Millie felt a chill run down her spine.

'That poor girl,' Cynthia said. 'She was only what? Twenty-three, twenty-four years old.'

'Yes, it's dreadful,' said Mrs Oaken-gate. 'And casts such a shadow over an otherwise lovely weekend.'

'Mrs Parker-Trent will be sorry she

put you out,' said Henry Fazeby.

'Oh, of course it's not her fault.' Mrs Oakengate had the grace to look embarrassed. 'But one does wonder how she could be so careless.'

'And Mr Parker-Trent?' said Barbara Conrad, casting an irritated glance at Mrs Oakengate.

'He is in great distress, as you can imagine, and doesn't wish to see anyone at the moment. Chlomsky has helped him to his room.'

'I think then that the best thing we can all do is go home,' Barbara said.

'That won't be possible,' said James Haxby, entering the room. 'Can I have some of that brandy, Henry? Thank you.' He drank it down in one go. His face was pale, but there was something else that Millie noticed. He looked furious.

'What do you mean, not possible?' said Mrs Oakengate. 'If I want to leave, I shall leave.'

'The police are on their way,' Haxby said, pouring another brandy. He looked as though he were about to drink that down too, but seemed to change his mind and sipped from it instead.

'Why?' Alex Markham turned to him. It was clearly news to him.

'Because just before she died, Mrs Parker-Trent told me that she'd been pushed.' Haxby looked round the room, searching every face for a reaction.

'No!' said Millie, feeling as if she might lose her equilibrium at any moment. The room seemed to swirl around her. It was even worse than she had imagined. 'That's awful. But who?'

'Did she give a name?' asked Barbara. She was sitting next to Millie, and had reached out her hand and placed it on Millie's arm, to steady her.

Everyone turned to Haxby, in expectation. Millie wondered if she were the only one considering it might be someone sitting in that very room.

'No,' said Haxby. 'No, she didn't mention any names.' Odd that he said names, thought Millie, and not a name.

'I asked her, 'how did you fall?' and she said 'Not fall. Pushed'. Then I asked her who, but she passed out.' Something in his face told Millie he was lying. No, not lying exactly, but holding something back. Then he looked directly at her, and she felt the colour rush to her face. Did he think she had done it?

'Excuse me, sir,' the butler said, entering the room and addressing Henry. 'There's a policeman at the door. A Detective Inspector Brady.'

'Is that Simon Brady?' asked Haxby.

'I've no idea, sir. I can ask.'

'No, I'll come along and find out for myself. I know Brady,' said Haxby by way of explanation to the others. 'If it's Simon Brady, he used to work in the West Indies. Good man, and good at his job. He'll soon get to the bottom of this.' He was just about to leave the room when he turned back. 'Millie, come with me. Inspector Brady may need to talk to you.'

Unable to refuse the request, but all

too aware of everyone's inquisitive glare, Millie followed Haxby out of the room.

'It is you!' he said, when they reached the hallway. He greeted Brady warmly. Brady was a good looking man, around Haxby's age, with a rugged complexion that spoke of a long time spent in a warm climate. The two men were instantly at ease with each other. 'May I introduce you to Miss Millicent Woodbridge. She'll be helping us with this.'

'Helping us?' said Brady, grinning. 'I know you've helped me in the past, Jim, but this isn't the colonies. We do things a bit more by the book here.'

'Of course we'll do it by the book. I just might interpret the text slightly differently to you.' He said it as if he would brook no argument. Brady looked at him levelly, before nodding.

'I've got nothing to do with this,' Millie said. 'I walked back down Masson Hill with you.' The words rushed out, leaving her breathless.

'It's all right, Millie. I know you

didn't.' Haxby looked almost amused by her outburst. They were shown to the library, where they could talk in private. The two men took a comfortable seat near the fire, whilst Millie sat on the sofa, still unsure of her role in all this.

'So,' said Brady, after exchanging the necessary pleasantries with Millie, 'Tell me about Hortense Parker-Trent. You say that she said something to you before she died, Jim?'

'Yes.' Haxby looked at Millie and smiled slightly. 'She told me that she was pushed. But she also told me something else. She said, 'I heard talking. Millie's father is innocent.''

'She didn't say who she heard talking?' asked Brady.

'No. The woman could hardly breathe, speaking took a lot of effort.'

'She told me last night, just before I met you on the stairs, that she had something to tell me,' said Millie. 'But Mr Parker-Trent wouldn't let her. He wouldn't let me talk to her today.'

'He wasn't kind to that girl,' said Haxby.

'So I've heard,' said Brady. 'Hortense is from around these parts, you know, and people still follow her progress. Rumour has it that marrying Parker-Trent wasn't the escape the poor girl thought it was going to be.'

'Do you think he pushed her?' asked Millie, horrified. 'To stop her talking to me? But why would he? Unless he was one the one she heard talking. But what would he know about my father?'

'That's what I intend to find out,' said Brady.

'Can we be there when you interview people?' asked Haxby.

'Jim, I've told you, this isn't the colonies. We have to do things by the book here. And, whilst I hate to say this, you and Miss Woodridge have to be treated as suspects.'

'No, because we're each other's alibi,' said Haxby. 'We walked down Masson Hill together, and never lost sight of each other until they came and told us about Mrs Parker-Trent. Isn't that so, Millie?'

'Yes,' said Millie. But her mind was thinking of something else. If Mrs Parker-Trent spoke her last words to Haxby, who was to say he didn't silence her?

'And what about when you were on the ledge with her, Haxby?' asked Brady. He looked at Millie and nodded, as if he had already guessed her train of thought.

'Oh come on, Simon,' said Haxby, his eyes flashing in anger. 'And you, Millie. You don't really believe . . . '

'No, I don't,' Simon said. 'I know why you're here, so you'd have no reason to silence Mrs Parker-Trent.'

'You do hear a lot,' said Haxby, smiling his easy smile.

'I make it my business to know everything that's happening.'

'Then I wish someone would tell me,' said Millie, 'so I can know too.'

'Millie,' said Haxby, 'I came here this weekend because I was asked to

64

investigate the possibility that someone in this house framed your father. Not only that but they intend to betray the country again. That's why it was a surprise to see you here.'

'Who? Chlomsky?'

'That's a possibility. The truth is we don't know. Only that our intelligence tells us that an important document was going to be handed over to an enemy agent at Fazeby Hall.'

'By a visitor? Not someone living here already?' said Millie. She could not imagine Henry and Cynthia Fazeby being involved in wrong-doing, but anything was possible.

'Actually that's a good point,' said Haxby. 'We don't know who is involved. So it could be anyone.'

'How do you know it's not me?' asked Millie.

'I pride myself on being a good judge of character. There's no way you'd have sent your own father to his death.'

'You don't know me. For all you know I may be cold and callous.'

'With those eyes? I don't think so.'

'Ahem,' said Simon Brady, grinning. 'Now we've established that Miss Woodridge's eyes preclude her from being a femme fatale, shall we concentrate on finding out who is guilty?'

★　★　★

Simon Brady, still refusing to let Millie and Haxby take part in the interviews, spoke to everyone who had visited Masson Hill that morning, but no one had seen anything.

Dinner that night was a sombre affair. Millie thought it was a testament to British upper-class fortitude that it took place at all. The world may be falling apart, but customs must be observed.

Mr Parker-Trent was the only guest absent. Inspector Brady left the Hall some time before, to continue with his investigations.

'I left Parker-Trent sleeping,' said Count Chlomsky when he joined them for an aperitif before dinner was served. 'It will be better for him to rest.'

'Yes, of course,' said Cynthia. 'I wish there were something we could do for the poor man.'

Millie was surprised by how hard Hortense's death had hit Parker-Trent. She would have sworn that he did not care for his silly young wife. On the other hand, he might see her as one of his possessions. Like his factory. Something to be held onto at all costs. Perhaps, Millie thought to herself, I'm being unfair. After all, one never knows the real truth about a marriage. Some neighbours near her old home were always arguing, to the point of the police being called to restore order. Yet they had celebrated fifty years of marriage that each described as 'happy' when the local newspaper covered the event. Perhaps even the Parker-Trents, too, had been happy in their own way.

Only Mrs Oakengate was unfazed by the sad event, and in a way, it helped to break the deadly silence. She regaled them with tales of her life on the stage.

'I was five years old when my mother first introduced me to the audience on Drury Lane,' she told them. 'I played Juliet at the age of fifteen.

By the time dinner had ended, she had reached her final performance. 'The audience cried when I told them that I was leaving to become a respectable married woman,' she said. 'I still get letters begging me to return to the stage.'

'Would you like to act in moving pictures?' asked Millie.

'Good Lord, no,' said Mrs Oakengate. 'It is a culturally bereft medium, and the actresses who star in such films nothing more than prostitutes.'

'Not like good old Nell Gwynne, then,' said James Haxby, winking at the other guests. Millie smiled into her coffee.

'Oh, that's different,' said Mrs Oakengate, 'she was the mistress of a king. Did I tell you about the time that old reprobate King Edward cast his eye on me? Lily Langtry was most put out.'

Everyone waited, to see if she would tell them of illicit meetings with the King, but that seemed to be the extent of her story. When that was over, she went back to the beginning, only the second time around she took her first steps onto the stage at the age of four and played Juliet at fourteen.

'Was that before or after Henry the Eighth cast his eye on you?' muttered Henry Fazeby. Mrs Oakengate glared at him, before appearing to remember he was her host and laughing girlishly.

Millie blushed for her employer. She was not used to people who said exactly what they thought. Her father would have cut his tongue out rather than cause offence, yet James Haxby and Henry Fazeby did not seem to care if what they said offended or not. She realised that came from status. Henry Fazeby was a rich landowner who, though he had no title himself, was descended from a noble family.

James Haxby was also rich, but there

was another reason for his bluntness. He had travelled, and faced terrible dangers. It made him fearless. Neither did he seem to care if people liked him, and as a result, people liked him very much. Millie wished she could be more like that.

'I think it's time we ladies left the men to their port,' said Cynthia. She turned to the butler. 'Jenkins, could you go and check on Mr Parker-Trent? Take him a tray, in case he's hungry.'

* * *

The women were just taking their coffee, when there was a commotion from the dining room. A few moments later the door to the drawing room opened and Henry Fazeby stood there, looking aghast.

'What is it, Henry?' asked Cynthia.

'It's Parker-Trent. He . . . he's dead.'

'His heart gave out,' the doctor told them, when they were all seated in the drawing room an hour later. The doctor was an elderly man who looked as if he should have retired some years previously. 'Not surprising really, given the shock he'd had today. He was on tablets for blood pressure, and I gather that Parker-Trent had already survived one heart attack.' He looked to Henry Fazeby for confirmation.

'Yes, that's correct. He told us about it last night, after the ladies had left us. Myself, Markham and Chlomsky, that is. Mr Haxby hadn't arrived yet.'

The doctor nodded. 'So, not surprising at all, although it's always sad with a husband and wife on the same day. I've known it happen, with a couple who have been together for a long time, but I gather they'd only been married a few months.'

'One does not need to know someone all one's life to become utterly devoted to them,' said Haxby. Yet he did not sound as though he believed that of the Parker-Trents anymore than Millie did.

'No, certainly,' said the doctor. 'It's

71

all very unfortunate.'

Millie glanced up, and realised that Haxby was looking at her. She wondered if he were thinking what she was thinking. That it might seem fortunate to someone in the household. If Hortense had shared information with her husband, it gave her killer a motive to want him out of the way.

'You are sure it was a heart attack?' asked Millie.

'I'm sure the doctor knows his job, Millicent,' snapped Mrs Oakengate, getting up from her chair. 'Really, child, you are in a contrary mood today. Come along to my room, I want to talk to you before we go to bed.'

'Let it wait until the morning,' said Barbara Conrad, looking at Millie kindly. 'It's been a long day and we're all upset.'

'Thank you, Mrs Conrad,' said Mrs Oakengate. 'But this is between myself and my employee.' Millie knew that was all she was; staff. She may have more freedom and status than serving staff, but in the end she was still a paid worker. Mrs Oakengate left the room, like a ship sailing through stormy seas.

'Goodnight, everyone,' said Millie, getting up to follow Mrs Oakengate.

'Millie,' said James Haxby.

'Yes?'

'I'd like a word in private.'

'Again,' said Cynthia Fazeby, with a hint of amusement in her voice. Millie noticed that she exchanged knowing glances with Barbara Conrad. It seemed that both women were in on a secret about which Millie had no knowledge.

Millie had the distinct feeling that talking to him in private would get her into more trouble with her employer. 'I really should go and see what Mrs Oakengate wants.'

'It won't take long.'

He followed Millie into the hallway, shutting the drawing room door behind him. 'I want you to lock your door tonight. Don't let anyone in. Even if you think you can trust them.'

'Why?'

'You and I both know that Parker-Trent's death wasn't by natural causes. He's dead because the person who killed his wife believes she may have told him what she was going to tell you. They may not know that she didn't get a chance to speak to you.'

'Doesn't that mean you're also in danger?' asked Millie. 'You were the last person she spoke to.'

'I can look after myself. It's you I'm worried about.' He said it with such tenderness that Millie once again felt her eyes sting. She stopped herself, feeling angry that so many times over the past couple of days she had come close to tears. She was not a weak person, and she despised women who burst out sobbing all the time, yet the small kindnesses that had been shown to her continually brought her to the brink of crying.

'I've had to look after myself for a while now,' said Millie. 'I'll be all right.'

'Yes. I rather believe you will, my grey lady.'

'Millicent!' Mrs Oakengate's imperious voice rang out from the gallery above the hallway. 'I said I wanted to speak to you forthwith.'

Millie turned to leave, but James caught her by the arm. 'Whatever she says, you've done nothing wrong.'

'I know. But I am an employee, so I must go.'

'That won't always be so, Millie. When all this is over . . . '

'Millicent. I will not tell you again!'

Millie whispered goodnight and turned to leave him, wondering what he was going to say next.

5

Half an hour passed before Millie was finally able to seek sanctuary in her own bedroom. She locked the door, not as a result of Haxby's warning, but due to a pressing desire to lock the world out — or Mrs Oakengate at the very least.

She had endured a lengthy lecture from her employer. 'Really, Millicent, the way you threw yourself at that man.'

'Which man?' Millie had asked, her cheeks aflame.

'Haxby, of course. Unless there are others I don't know about. I daresay that like many young girls you find him exciting, but you must know he is not for the likes of you. I don't say this unkindly,' Mrs Oakengate paused, as if garnering her strength. 'But you are a plain girl, with no real attributes. The sort of woman who would excite James Haxby would have seen something of the world. She would be older, sophisticated, and not, I am sorry to say, the daughter of an executed spy.

'Now, I will forgive you your behaviour today, but should you disobey me again, you will find yourself out of a job. I do not need to remind you that you would find great difficulty in finding other employment with an upper class employer, given your status. No, you and I are stuck with each other, through my loyalty to your dear mother. So we must make the best of it. And we can only do that if you clear your mind of any silly notions of finding a man who will want to marry you.'

The memory of Mrs Oakengate's dressing down caused Millie to fall onto her bed, beating her fists into her pillow. If only she had Haxby's courage. If only she had any courage. The growing fear that Mrs Oakengate was right gripped her like a vice, constricting her, knocking the breath right out of her.

Millie had no 'silly notions', as Mrs

Oakengate called them, of being married. She tried not to consider that marriage to Haxby might be very exciting. It might be exhilarating to be in his company, given that he was such a force of nature, but she had no illusions about him.

And yet, he had aroused feelings in her she never knew she had. Yearnings for something she was afraid to name, but which made her body tingle at the thought of his touch. Had she really thrown herself at him? She blushed to think it might be so. He probably despised her for it every bit as much as Mrs Oakengate did, whilst encouraging her — perhaps because it flattered his ego — with a kindness and tenderness she had not known since her father's death.

The worst part was that what Mrs Oakengate said about her not finding other employment might well be true. How then could she live? It was then that Millie realised she was neither a proud nor a snobbish person. She would happily work in a factory or a shop, rather than suffer years of humiliation at the hands of Mrs Oakengate. She had seen the factory girls on the streets near to her old home. They had often looked exhausted at the end of their shift, but they also possessed, in their countenance, a look of freedom that she now lacked.

She paced her floor, long into the night, working out if it would be possible to just leave Mrs Oakengate. She would have to give notice, and that was the part that worried her. She suspected Mrs Oakengate would simply brush the resignation aside, and carry on as if nothing had changed. To run away might be her only chance of avoiding years as Mrs Oakengate's charity case. She would have to leave a note, so no one would try to send the police after her, as they might do if she just disappeared.

She realised she could not go anywhere until the investigation into Hortense Parker-Trent's death had ended. They might think she was running away because she was guilty. Besides, she wanted to know the answer herself. Who had pushed Hortense off the cliff? Was her husband's death really a heart attack, due to immense grief? Who had Hortense heard speaking about Millie's father? The thought that someone in the house was a murderer disturbed Millie greatly.

Unable to sleep, Millie picked up Barbara Conrad's manuscript, and tried to read a few paragraphs. It was very well written, and Barbara had a way of deftly showing the idiosyncrasies of human nature. Despite that, Millie could not concentrate. She put it back on her bedside table, and lay down, thinking long into the night. About the two deaths, about escape, about freedom from Mrs Oakengate's condescension.

But her last unbidden thought, before drifting into a dreamless sleep, was about James Haxby and how his lips might feel against hers.

★   ★   ★

'Millie, Simon Brady and I are going back up to Masson Hill this morning. Would you like to come with us? Another pair of eyes might be very useful.'

The breakfast table fell into silence as if the answer mattered to everyone.

'I'm afraid I must stay here,' said Millie, looking down at her plate regretfully. She would have liked nothing more than to go with the two men and help in their investigations, and felt a small thrill at being asked. 'Mrs Oakengate needs me.'

'Yes, that is true,' said Mrs Oakengate. 'Besides, it is not seemly for a young woman to go off in the company of two men.'

'Did you think I intended to seduce her whilst Brady watched?' asked Haxby. He threw down his napkin and rose from the table. 'I may have visited some savage places,' he said, angrily, 'but I have never been accused of behaving like a savage.'

'Might I remind you, Mr Haxby,' said Mrs Oakengate in her sweetest, deadliest voice, 'that Millicent is employed by me as my companion, and as such is subject to my commands.'

'And don't you just love that?' said Haxby angrily. 'Ordering that girl around, questioning her worth in this world. Telling her whom she might or might not love.'

Millie gasped. Had he followed and listened to the conversation of the night before? If so, why would he? Perhaps he suspected her or Mrs Oakengate of some wrong-doing. Or perhaps he had merely guessed what her employer would say to her.

'Haxby . . . ' Henry Fazeby's voice was gentle, but firm. 'You are not really helping Miss Woodgate's cause. Or your own.'

Haxby had too much respect for Fazeby to argue back. He merely nodded and murmured an apology, aimed at Millie, before leaving the room.

'James has spent so long abroad, he sometimes forgets the niceties of English manners,' said Cynthia. 'You must forgive

him, Victoria.' Millie sensed an underlying plea to Mrs Oakengate to forgive
Millie too, or perhaps it was just wishful
thinking on her part.

'Forgive him? Why, there is nothing
to forgive. I understand men like Haxby,'
said Mrs Oakengate, with an excited
gleam in her eyes. 'He must be master
of all he surveys. Of course, he would
never be my master, no man could. He
obviously thinks about me constantly,
don't you think? The way he takes such
an interest in my dealings with my young
charge here. That's why Henry had to
warn him to behave, isn't it, Henry?
Showing such passion publicly is unseemly,
even if it is all rather exciting.'

'Yes, of course, Victoria,' said Henry,
his mouth turning up slightly at the
corners. 'I knew there must be some
reason I said it.'

The morning passed by interminably
for Millie. Henry Fazeby was out on
the estate, talking to his manager, and
Alexander Markham had gone into the
town, having volunteered to deal with

the particulars involving the funerals of Mr and Mrs Parker-Trent. Count Chlomsky said he was going for a walk, but did not divulge his destination or when he would return.

Mrs Oakengate had very little use for Millie at all, having Barbara Conrad and Cynthia Fazeby for company in the drawing room. She filled up Millie's time with errands.

'Did I say my red scarf, Millicent? I'm sure I said my blue scarf.'

'You said your red scarf,' Barbara said, looking up from her book.

'No, I think you're mistaken. Besides, it is Millicent's job to remember these things, not yours, though it's very kind of you to take an interest.'

'No, not that book, the one in my other bag.' Her various commands ensured that Millie got plenty of exercise, and could at least eke out the errands so that she could spend at least ten minutes alone.

It was on one of many errands to fetch Mrs Oakengate's favourite slippers

— 'No, not the pink pair, the ones with the pearl appliqué. Honestly Millicent, you are in a dream world today.' — that Millie saw an unfamiliar man coming out of one of the bedrooms. His face was turned away from her, but there was something familiar about his gait.

Despite thinking that it was probably just one of the servants, Millie ducked back into a recess and watched his reflection in a mirror at the end of the hall as he went furtively across the landing into several bedrooms, appearing to spend some time searching, before going back to the original door. As she was watching through a reflected image, Millie found it difficult to gauge which rooms he targeted.

At first she thought he might be one of the police officers, sent to investigate, but she felt sure that Cynthia Fazeby would have mentioned it to them, and would have a servant overlooking the search. Only when he looked up briefly did Millie see in the mirror that he was the man with the pock-marked face that she had seen climbing Masson Hill.

She wondered who he was and what he hoped to find. He did not look like a policeman, and was not familiar with the layout of Fazeby Hall. He often went back into the same rooms then came out again, looking irritated by his mistake. It was with some shock that Millie realised his reflection in the mirror was moving towards her. At any moment, her hiding place in the recess would be revealed to him, and who knew what he might do when he found her spying on him?

She rushed back to her room, and shut the door, locking it from the inside. Just as she suspected, a few minutes later, someone tried to turn the handle. Millie held her breath, wondering if the man would go so far as to break the door down. He didn't. He walked away, and Millie heard him talking to someone. She would have liked to see who his companion was, but she was afraid to leave her room whilst the man was still in the vicinity.

Millie waited five minutes, pacing her floor, wondering who the man was and why he was searching the rooms, and then, after locking her bedroom door from the outside, started to make her way back to the drawing room. She had reached the top of the stairs when the man once again exited one of the bedrooms, and stood watching her as she descended. She hoped that he had not realised she was there all along.

Her heart beat rapidly, wishing that Haxby were returned so she could tell him about the man. She strongly believed there was some connection between the man being at Masson Hill the day before, and him searching the rooms at Fazeby Hall. Wondering if she should tell Cynthia Fazeby, she went back to the drawing room.

'Where have you been, child?' said Mrs Oakengate.

'I had trouble finding them,' Millie said, surprised by how easily the lie fell from her lips. She would not have called herself a dishonest person. 'Mrs

Fazeby, I wonder . . . there was a man upstairs. Is he a member of your staff? I only ask because I had not seen him before. His face is pock-marked.'

'I hardly think it kind to draw attention to peoples' shortcomings, Millicent,' said Mrs Oakengate. 'Especially when one has little to recommend oneself.'

'I think Millie is very pretty,' Barbara Conrad said, glancing up from reading her magazine.

'Do you really?' asked Mrs Oakengate.

'I believe that's Vasily, Count Chlomsky's valet,' Cynthia cut in quickly, before the argument about Millie's attributes became too heated. 'He only arrived last night, having had business in London for the Count.'

Millie wondered whether to say the man had been searching the rooms, but did not get a chance.

'It is hard to get good valets nowadays, I believe,' said Mrs Oakengate. 'I blame socialism. Do you know I got into a taxicab the other day, and the driver called me 'duckie'. he said he'd lost his leg during the war, but that's hardly an excuse for bad manners. That would never have happened during Queen Victoria's time.'

The return of James Haxby and Simon Brady put an end to Mrs Oakengate's reminiscences and prevented Millie from having to explain her interest in Count Chlomsky's valet. Her only regret was in being unable to get Haxby alone and tell him what she had seen.

Just before lunch Alexander Markham returned, as did Henry Fazeby. Only Chlomsky was missing. 'We've had word that he's returned to London,' said Henry, as they awaited the luncheon bell. 'His valet was here this morning, packing the Count's luggage.'

'I thought no one was allowed to leave,' said Mrs Oakengate.

'Unfortunately,' said Simon Brady, who had been invited to join them for luncheon, 'his diplomatic status means we cannot stop him.'

'It's a strange thing,' said Millie, choosing her words carefully, and directing them at Haxby and Brady, 'but I was sure I saw Count Chlomsky's valet on Masson Hill yesterday, only it couldn't have been, because Mrs Fazeby tells me he only arrived last night.'

'Then it's hardly a story worth telling, is it?' said Mrs Oakengate. 'Millicent, I think we already had a discussion about your need to feel important. Do I have to remind you?'

Millie looked down at her lunch, but had lost her appetite.

'Simon,' said Haxby, 'I'd like to go up to London after lunch. Can you give me leave?'

'Certainly, as long as you tell me your whereabouts.'

'Of course. I'd like to take Millie with me.'

'Most certainly not,' said Mrs Oakengate. 'It's improper.'

'I believe we're in the twentieth century,' said Cynthia, 'where young women no longer need a chaperone, Victoria. I'm sure you can spare her for a few hours.' There was a firmness in

her voice that Millie had not hear
before. Millie wondered briefly if he
hostess would be glad to be rid of her,
yet the lady's eyes looked on her with
generosity.

'Then that's settled. We'll leave on
the afternoon train,' said Haxby. Mrs
Oakengate opened her mouth to
protest, but faced with Haxby's hard
stare, clamped it shut again.

6

Millie spent the next couple of hours feeling both awkward and excited. Awkward because Mrs Oakengate kept giving her dark looks. Excited because she would be going to London with Haxby. Why he should choose to take her, she did not know, but she had no intentions of arguing. If Mrs Oakengate dismissed her, it would at least give Millie the impetus she needed to start living her own life, free from restraints set by others.

She believed her life had begun a course over which she had no control. Where it might lead, she did not know, but she had never felt so alive, so stimulated. She began to understand why Haxby spent his life seeking excitement. But along with that understanding came the nagging doubt and fear that she was simply not interesting enough for such a man.

No sooner had lunch ended, than a

car was brought around, and they set off for the station. At first, Millie could barely speak, despite the questions that filled her mind. Being alone with Haxby, albeit with a chauffeur in the front seat, rendered her speechless. They exchanged a few pleasantries about the weather and about how charming their hosts were, but discussed nothing of the impending trip.

It was only when they were seated in a first class carriage, on route to London, that Millie finally found to courage to ask, 'Why did you bring me?'

'Because you know what this Vasily looks like.'

'So does Mrs Fazeby.'

'Yes, but I rather think Henry might protest if I ran off with his wife.'

Millie could not help smiling. 'No one would blame you. She is lovely.'

'So are you — and you have the added benefit of not being married to another man.'

Unused to men paying her compliments, Millie could only gaze out of the window, barely seeing the fields and factories they passed. 'Do you think Vasily was the man who killed Mrs Parker-Trent?' she asked, finding safer ground on which to tread.

'I have a feeling you do.'

Millie nodded. 'I saw him as we were walking down the hill. At the time, I only noticed him because of his bad skin condition, which was very unkind of me. But there's more to it than you know. This morning, I saw him going through each of the upper rooms in Fazeby Hall. He was looking for something, I'm sure of it.'

Haxby's eyes widened. 'Does anyone else know this?'

'No, I didn't know who he was at the time and thought he might be one of the policemen. Then I saw his face and recognised him. I grew really suspicious when Cynthia — Mrs Fazeby — said he had only arrived last night. He may have only arrived at Fazeby Hall then, but I know he's the man I saw in the morning.'

'Now the Count has fled to London,'

said Haxby. 'He should be quite easy to find. He'll have gone straight to his Embassy. We'll watch there for a while, to see if Vasily arrives.'

'Then what?'

'Then I'm going to question him, and find out exactly what he was doing on Masson Hill yesterday.'

'Oh.' Despite her misgivings, Millie found the whole thing very exciting, as if she had fallen into one of the exciting spy stories she used to read to her father. She reminded herself that such stories seldom ended with the execution of innocent men, and that memory brought her sadness, and a sense of guilt that she should be enjoying this adventure so much.

Haxby reached across the carriage and took her hand in his. 'I think we'll be able to prove your father was innocent of all charges.'

'To what end?' said Millie, her eyes glistening with unshed tears. 'A posthumous pardon is of little use to my father.'

'But it may be of use to you in restoring your status, and you may be able to claim some compensation for your loss. Then you can tell Mrs Oakengate to go to hell. Sorry,' he sat back in his seat. 'I forget how to behave in front of ladies sometimes.'

Millie had to admit that the thought of being able to live independently was an attractive one, but the cost for her had already been too high. A sum of money might make her life easier, but she would always know that it came out of her father's misfortune. 'I don't care about money,' she said, speaking in all honesty. 'But I do care about clearing my father's name.'

'Good. Who knows, you might then settle down and marry some boring little bank clerk.'

'You mean I will be a suitable wife then,' said Millie, with more bitterness than she intended. 'Yes, I suppose I shall. It's just a pity that I would rather marry someone who did not care a jot either way, and who loved me enough for it not to matter to him, so I shall probably never marry.'

'Unfortunately we live in a world where such things do matter,' said Haxby. 'Particularly when there has been a war where millions of young men lost their lives. If people believe that your father is guilty of hastening their end, by sharing our secrets, it will be hard for them to forgive and forget. It's unjust, but the sins of the father, and all that . . . '

Millie felt her heart sink and her enthusiasm for their adventure wane. Even when she believed he may just be trying to seduce her, she had secretly hoped that he would turn out to have feelings for her, despite her family ignominy. Now she knew that whilst he may briefly desire her, his status would always prevent anything further between them. Haxby sighed. 'And now I've hurt you, which is the last thing I wanted to do.'

'No, you've spoken the truth, and I'm grateful for it. In the words of Mrs

Oakengate I was getting ideas above my station. You have successfully cured me of that.' What a silly girl you are, she thought to herself, staring out of the window and avoiding his searching gaze for the rest of the trip.

7

Most of Millie's worries were swept up in the excitement of their arrival in London. Being in the capital always enthralled her; the hustle and bustle of traffic where horses and carriages still shared space with new motorcars; the noise of the barkers on roadside stalls and the elegant young women who went about the important business of being elegant young women. They had poise and confidence that Millie envied. She could not help noticing the glances they cast in James Haxby's direction and fancied that their gazes hardened when they saw the mousey woman walking next to him. Every one of them would have made a more suitable companion.

They took a taxi cab to the Ritz Hotel where Haxby booked them rooms next door to each other. Millie had assumed they would return to Derbyshire that evening. She also assumed that they would go to Chlomsky's embassy to keep watch, only to learn that Haxby had contacted a detective agency, who kept watch on their behalf.

'We'll have dinner here, then the agent is going to come along and report his findings,' said Haxby, before they were each shown to their room.

'I thought we'd be the ones watching,' said Millie.

'That's hardly wise. Chlomsky knows us.'

'But you said that you needed me to identify Vasily.'

'Oh, I do. I do.' His manner was vague. 'Come, we'll change for dinner, and I'll meet you in the restaurant.' It seemed to Millie that Haxby once again held something back. His manner became vague.

Millie was embarrassed to admit that she had nothing to change into. 'I wasn't expecting to stay the night,' she said. All she had brought with her was a small bag, containing a few toilet items and Barbara Conrad's novel, which she had intended to read on the train. Even that gave her a pang of guilt, as she had not asked, telling herself that it would not matter, since she intended to return to Fazeby Hall.

Haxby looked her up and down appraisingly, then said, 'Don't worry, I know a woman who can take care of that. Go and freshen up, and someone will come to you.'

Half an hour later, Millie answered a knock at her door and admitted a middle aged woman, with a motherly air. Behind her stood a porter, carrying a large trunk.

'Hello, Miss, I'm Mrs Turner, a friend of Mr Haxby's. I've brought some particulars for you, Miss.'

The archaic term made Millie smile. Mrs Turner ordered the porter to leave the luggage. It was with further embarrassment that Millie realised she had not given him a tip. 'Mr Haxby will take care of that,' said Mrs Turner, as if reading her mind. 'Now, let me look at you. Oh, yes, if Mr Haxby knows anything it's women's sizes.'

'Does he?' said Millie, standing in the middle of the room, whilst Mrs Turner took her measurements. 'Do you . . . em . . . do you do this for him with a lot of ladies?'

'I'm sure I shouldn't gossip,' said Mrs Turner. 'Don't slump your shoulders, dear. But yes, he has used my services more than once.'

'I see.' Millie's face flushed with shame. No doubt Mrs Turner thought of Millie as just another notch in Haxby's bedpost. She wondered if everyone in the hotel thought the same. What on earth had she walked into?

'I think, on reflection,' said Millie, trying to regain some pride, 'that I'll wear my own clothes after all.'

'I'm sure it's a very nice dress, Miss,' said Mrs Turner, eyeing Millie's grey tweed pinafore doubtfully, 'but hardly suitable for dinner at the Ritz. Let me show you what I've brought, and if there's nothing you like I'll send for something else.'

Millie fully expected to be presented with clothes more suitable to a lady of the night, so she was pleasantly surprised to see that Mrs Turner had brought along clothes that were similarly elegant to those worn by other young ladies in London. She settled for a dress of ivory Brussels lace, which settled on her curves as if it had been designed with her in mind.

'Oh, you're a picture, Miss. A real picture,' said Mrs Turner. 'I've seen lots of young ladies wearing that dress, but none as delightfully as you.'

Millie's pleasure was momentarily abated by the thought that another of Haxby's lovers had also worn the same dress. The words lamb to the slaughter crossed her mind. He would hardly seduce her in a restaurant full of people but the idea that these same people — the staff at least — would be used to him courting many other young women in public was too painful to contemplate.

And afterwards, when they returned to their rooms . . . Millie tried not to think of it.

With a matching scarf around her shoulders as some security against the low cut of the neckline and her hair brushed to a luscious shine, she eventually made her way downstairs to the restaurant, to find Haxby already waiting for her.

Looking devastatingly handsome in a black tuxedo, he drew admiring glances from many of the women present. Oblivious to the equally admiring glances she received from the men, Millie joined him.

'Well . . . ' he said, as he helped her to her seat, 'I'm seldom rendered speechless, but for once I don't know what to say.' As she sat down, and he pushed her chair under her, she felt his mouth softly against her hair, sending a thrill through her whole body. 'You look exquisite,' he whispered.

Millie blushed, but any awkwardness she felt in replying was, thankfully, taken up with the process of ordering dinner.

'And champagne, I think,' Haxby said to the waiter, closing his menu after they had chosen.

'My father brought me here once for afternoon tea,' said Millie, just for something to say.

'Everyone should have tea at the Ritz at least once in their lifetime,' said Haxby. 'My mother used to bring me here whenever we visited Britain.'

'You weren't brought up here?'

'No, my family were old colonials. I was born in the West Indies. Then my father became an ambassador and we moved around a lot.'

'Is that why you seldom stay in one place for long now?'

'Yes, I suppose it is,' said Haxby. 'There isn't anywhere I can call home.'

'Yet your loyalties are to Britain.'

'Of course. One never forgets the mother country. When I'm too old for travelling, I fancy I'll move to Kent, keep a few goats.' Millie laughed at the idea of Haxby as a farmer. 'Oh, you may mock, young Millie, but a man has to have something to keep him going into his old age.'

'You don't think you'll ever marry then?' Millie regretted asking the moment she said it.

'I'd make a terrible husband,' he replied. 'After all, what woman would want to spend her whole life travelling? They want a home, children, with a grocer on the corner.'

'Your mother travelled, from what you say.'

'My mother was — is — an exceptional woman, and there are few like her.'

'Where is she now? Still travelling?'

'No, she owns a farm in Kent — keeps a few goats.' He smiled. 'Honestly. That's why I know it's where I'll retire.'

'Meanwhile you just want excitement and glamour.'

'Oh, glamour isn't worth having. It's too transient and the public's idea of it changes from year to year. But excitement, yes, most certainly. My biggest fear is boredom.'

Millie was tempted to ask him why on earth he was sitting in the Ritz with her. Instead she lapsed into silence as they ate their starter. 'Mr Haxby . . . '

'I think we can dispense with that now. Call me Jim.'

She could not explain to him that it was the last thing she wanted to call him. Had he not told her that women called him that when they became intimate with him? To do so would be to admit that she wanted to be on those terms with him, to feel his arms around her, to know how it felt to . . .

'Do you really care about clearing my father's name? Or is this whole thing just your way of getting me into your bed?' The question came out far more savagely than Millie intended. It was the only way she could armour herself against his searching eyes, which appeared to be looking right through the thin fabric she wore.

'Now what brought that on?' To Millie's surprise he laughed. It made her feel even worse, because he clearly saw her as a thing of amusement.

'It was Mrs Turner telling me how often she'd taken care of the ladies you bring to the Ritz. Really, I wonder that so few of them possess the correct attire.'

Haxby threw down his knife and fork, causing several other diners to look over at them. He hissed across the table, 'Millie, despite what you obviously think, I am not in the habit of bringing women here to seduce them. I work for a government agency. I have often had call to bring new female agents here, and coach them in how to behave in such surroundings. It's a fact of our work that those women willing to take on the danger are not always able to fit into any society. Do you understand?' He said the last words as though speaking to a ten-year old.

'Yes,' she said, her head bowed in shame.

'I assure you that I have no intention

whatsoever of seducing you, now or at any other time.'

He might just as well have slapped her in the face. To learn that his intentions were entirely honourable would have been one thing. It would have removed some of the strain of being alone with him. But to learn that he in no way found her desirable, or ever would, filled her with despair.

How she managed to eat the food the waiter placed in front of her, she did not know. At the back of her mind was the idea that it would be sinful to waste such expensive food. She ate mechanically, because it was something to do that prevented her from having to speak to him.

They were on dessert when a man arrived and joined them at their table.

'This is Mister Barraclough. He's a private detective,' Haxby informed Millie. His manner had returned to normal, as if the previous exchange had not taken place. 'Barraclough, this is Miss Millicent Woodridge.'

Barraclough was a coarse looking man, who looked as uncomfortable in the Ritz as Millie felt. His stiff collar had left a red mark on his neck, which he kept rubbing. He was a man who clearly had little time for pleasantries, merely nodding at Millie. 'We found Vasily, but unfortunately he gave us the slip,' Barraclough explained. 'He ran into a music hall, and got lost amongst the crowd.'

'So you've no idea where he is now?' said Haxby.

'Oh, yes, we've managed to track him to a house in Wimbledon. I've just come along to ask what you want to do next. Don't worry, one of my men is still watching it.'

'What have you managed to find out about him?'

Barraclough took out a shabby notebook and began reading from its pages. 'He's only worked for Chlomsky for a few weeks. He was hired by some agency abroad, when Chlomsky's own valet got run over by a car.'

'Was it an accident?' asked Millie, her mind turning to ideas she could not yet fathom.

'There's no way we'll ever find out, Miss. It happened at the Embassy, which as you know, is sovereign land. They keep things to themselves.'

Haxby called the waiter for the bill, and said, 'I'll come along presently, Barraclough. Get back there and make sure you don't lose him again.' He turned to Millie and said, 'I'll see you to your room.'

'Am I not coming with you? I thought you wanted me to identify him.'

'I don't think that will be necessary now. Besides, I don't want to put you in any danger.'

Millie was about to say that it was hardly worth her making the trip to London, but thought better of it. Clearly Haxby was disappointed with her. She wondered if he had meant to seduce her, as a means of amusement to make the time pass more quickly, and he was angry that she had seen through his plans.

'Will you let me know what happens?' asked Millie, when she reached her room door. She stopped and turned to face him. Haxby was a few feet behind her, having fallen into a contemplative silence. 'With Vasily, I mean.'

'Of course. I'll come and see you when I get back. If you're sure I won't be compromising you.'

'I'm a big girl,' said Millie, not entirely sure that was true. With him she felt like a silly schoolgirl. He was so self-assured, so arrogant in many ways. 'I can look after myself.'

'Can you, Millie?' he asked, his eyes searching hers. He pulled her into his arms, the heat from his hands searing through her thin dress. Then his lips were on hers, and he crushed her to him. All the fight went out of her as she succumbed to his touch. 'Making love to you would be very easy,' he murmured against her throat. It should have made her come to her senses. She should have slapped his face and punished him for his arrogance. Instead she put her head against his shoulder, her lips trying to form an invitation she could not put into words. Little did she know that the invite was already written in her body and the way it yielded to him. She wanted him to go on kissing her and for the fingers that stroked her spine to keep working their magic. 'I have to go,' he said, kissing her again, then abruptly pushing her away. 'I'll come to you later.'

It was only after a few minutes alone in her hotel room that Millie came to her senses. What had he said? That making love to her would be easy? Was that what he thought of her? Her face burned with shame over her own behaviour. For a few moments she had lost her senses and had he come into her room with her at that time, she had no doubt she would have given in to his desires. She felt grateful that he had to leave. It gave her time to regain her strength.

Feeling she had no choice but to leave before he returned, Millie quickly changed her clothes and snatched up the simple bag of items she had brought with her. She hoped that he would take care of paying for the room, though doubtless he would feel he had a bad return on his investment.

'How can you have behaved so stupidly?' she said to her reflection in the mirror. 'Falling for his line about training women agents!' It was no doubt the line he gave to all the women he seduced. That and the fact he did not really require her help in finding Vasily. He had seen an opportunity and taken it. That was all.

Where to go, that was the problem. She felt too ashamed to return to Mrs Oakengate at the Fazebys, even if she could get a train. The late hour at which she arrived back would damn her in their eyes, and even if she were to stress there had been no untoward behaviour on her part, it was possible they would believe that Haxby had used her and cast her out straight away. Respectable girls did not return home in the early hours of the morning. At the back of her mind lay the truth that respectable girls did not go off to London with practical strangers, and end up spending the night, so either way she would have to face their disapproval.

She thought of the little town to the north of London, where she had lived with her father. They had some friends there, people who, even after his death, looked upon her kindly. There was a boarding house in the market square, and she had some money in the bank, not having much cause to spend the wage Mrs Oakengate paid her.

Suddenly the thought of returning home consumed her. After her father's death, she had been relieved to move away but now she missed home. She remembered Alex Markham's offer to help her financially; not that she would give in and marry him, but perhaps she should not have been so proud.

She knew now that she would never

marry. Her heart and soul were with Haxby, despite the fact that he only saw her as a conquest. Nowhere on earth would she find a man who excited her as he did, or with whom she would fall as deeply in love. Better to be alone than settle for second best, either by being Haxby's mistress, or by marrying another man.

Not for the first time, Millie missed her father. When they had each other, life seemed easy. Now she was struck by how completely alone she was, and she fought to stop the tears that had been building up for several days. She sighed impatiently, annoyed with herself for acting like such a weak-willed girl. She promised herself that when she returned home to her own town, she would once again find the strength she used to have. But first she had to leave the Ritz.

It did not occur to her until she was in the lift how hard it would be to walk away from Haxby. She had thought that once she was resolved to go, her decision would make it easier. But every step away from him was like a dagger in her heart. And not just from him, but from the situation regarding the Parker-Trents. Her loyalty to her father tore her in two. On the one hand, she failed him in not clearing his name. On the other hand, if she stayed, then she might shame his memory in other ways. She would not be the daughter he had raised; a girl with a sense of dignity and decorum, who would not succumb to the charms of a roué, no matter how fascinating and handsome he was.

She had walked along several streets in the night air before she realised that there was a third choice. She could return to the hotel, but refuse Haxby's advances, insisting he merely tell her what he had found out about Vasily, and his part in her father's downfall. She remembered his sensual touch, and her resolve failed her briefly. Then she turned and began walking back to the Ritz. She would face Haxby, as an adult with a mind of her own and not a silly schoolgirl who ran away at the idea of being seduced. She would clear her father's name, whilst still honouring his memory.

Her resolve became a blur as an arm reached out to her from the darkness, viciously grabbing her around the neck and pressing a sweet, sickly smelling cloth to her lips. She was vaguely aware of a familiar voice shouting, at which point everything fell into blackness.

8

The first thing of which Millie became aware was the morning sun streaming through bright curtains. Her second discovery, on trying to move her arms, was that she was not restrained in any way. All that covered her was a soft eiderdown. Finally, when she tried to move the rest of her body, a searing pain filled her head. It was then she realised that a bandage bound her forehead. Still, sleepy, she dozed slightly, opening her eyes when she heard voices.

'She doesn't look like the others.'

'She's not like the others.' She knew the second voice. It was Haxby.

Her mind became a whirl of confusion and she kept her eyes closed so he would not realise she could hear him. Had he abducted her? No, that did not make sense. She had been at his mercy all the time they were on the train, then again at the Ritz. Why would he need to abduct her from a late night street? Unless he wanted to be sure no one could connect him to her abduction. He had an alibi in that he left the hotel at around ten o'clock to go with Barraclough. No, none of it made sense and it hurt her, both physically and emotionally to think of the consequences of it being true.

'If you're lying there wondering if I kidnapped you, the answer is no,' he said. Millie opened her eyes and looked up at him. He seemed taller than ever, towering above the bed. Next to him stood a woman of indiscriminate age. Nearly as tall as Haxby and with grey hair coiled on her head and wearing an old-fashioned morning dress; she might have been seventy, yet her eyes held the energy of a twenty year old, bright and intelligent, and, Millie guessed, missing very little.

Millie tried to get up, only to fall back, as dizziness overwhelmed her. 'Be careful,' Haxby said gently, sitting on

120

the edge of the bed. 'You hit your head on a pillar box when you fell.'

'What happened?' She tentatively touched her forehead, and met a large and very painful bump.

'Vasily managed to get out of the house we were watching without being seen. Luckily I was on my way back to the Ritz when I saw him attack you.'

'But why?'

'Enough questions for now,' said the woman. 'You'll tire yourself out, child. James Thomas Haxby, the very least you can do after turning up at my home in the early hours is to introduce me properly.'

'Of course. Where are my manners? Mother, this is Millie . . . Miss Millicent Woodridge . . . Millie, this is my mother, Helen Haxby.'

Millie tried to raise her hand, but again was overcome with weakness.

'Don't worry about the formalities, child,' said Helen, leaning over and patting Millie's arm. 'I'm very glad to meet you. Now, Jim, let the girl rest, while you come downstairs and tell me what on earth is going on.'

'I'd rather like to stay with Millie, mother.'

'I'm sure you would, but I'm still old-fashioned enough to believe that a young lady should never be alone in her bedroom with a man. You should certainly not be alone with this particular young lady, anyway.' With that, she left the room, with Haxby following meekly behind. Millie thought she heard him mutter something about 'Why not her?' Millie could have told him. Despite Helen's kindness, which probably came down to no more than good breeding, she no doubt disapproved of her son being associated with the daughter of a traitor.

She would have liked to go downstairs with them, to learn for herself what was happening, and why Vasily had tried to snatch her, but finding herself once again thrown into despair about her status, she preferred to pull the eiderdown over her head and shut the cruel world out.

Millie eventually joined them downstairs in the evening. Whatever Helen Haxby's private misgivings might have been, she hid them well, treating Millie like an honoured guest.

'Are you comfortable, child? Would you prefer a chair nearer to the fire?'

'I'm quite well, thank you,' said Millie, lost in the corner of a large overstuffed sofa. Haxby sat next to her, too close.

For some reason, Millie had imagined Helen Haxby's home to be a smallholding, with geese and chickens in the back yard. The reality was a Georgian manor of immense proportions. She had been given a quick tour of the house and grounds. The land that James described as a 'farm' probably ran to several hundred acres.

'Will you tell me what happened now?' she said to Haxby, as she sipped a cup of tea and nibbled on the slice of buttered toast that Helen had insisted on making for her. 'Why did Vasily try to abduct me?'

'I was hoping that you could tell me that,' said Haxby. 'I thought it might be because he thought Hortense Parker-Trent had managed to tell you something, but you've had plenty of opportunities to impart that information to others since her death.'

'Was there anything your father ever said to you?' asked Helen. 'Any work that he shared with you?'

'He shared all his work with me,' said Millie. 'But I wouldn't tell the enemy. Neither would my father.'

'No, of course not,' said Helen. 'Unfortunately the enemy have ways of getting such information. It's lucky Jim happened along when he did.'

'Where is Vasily now?' asked Millie.

Haxby and his mother exchanged glances. 'He's dead,' said Haxby.

'You killed him?'

'I would have liked to, for what he tried to do to you, but sadly he took that pleasure from me. We had him in our grasp, but he took a cyanide pill before we could get any information from him. Then I brought you here.'

'Why here? Why not Fazeby Hall? Not that I'm ungrateful for your hospitality Mrs Haxby,' Millie added hastily.

'There's something going on there,' said Haxby. 'I don't want you in any more danger than you have been already. I thought I made a mistake taking you to London. Now I realise it was probably safer in the long run. At least until Vasily found out you were there. And the only way he could have known that was if someone at Fazeby Hall told him.'

'But how did he know I was leaving the Ritz?' asked Millie.

'He probably had someone watching the place, waiting for an opportunity. Which reminds me. Why did you leave?' He turned to look at her and, to make matters worse, Helen Haxby also appeared to be eagerly awaiting her answer.

'I just wanted some fresh air.'

'At that time of night? It was very

foolish. For God's sake, Millie, who knows what might have happened to you?'

'I'm guessing that Millie thought it safer to leave,' said Helen Haxby, her eyes exuding owl-like wisdom.

'Oh, I see.' Haxby left the room, his face gripped by an emotion Millie could not identify. She stared into the fire, not knowing what to say.

'Don't mind Jim's bad mood,' said Helen. 'For a man who believes he always says what he really thinks, my son can be rather obtuse when it matters. In my experience, most men are the same. The truth is that he was worried sick about you. I'd never seen him as upset as when he arrived here with you this morning.'

'You . . . ' Millie paused, choosing her words carefully. 'You said I'm not like the others. What did you mean?'

'I don't know how much Jim has told you about his work for the government. He — actually we — train young women for the secret service. Unfortunately most of the women who have the intelligence and courage to do the work often lack the social graces that would allow them to fit into any society. Those who do have the social graces are often complete airheads. So the intelligent but less graceful girls come and live here for a while, and I teach them the basics.'

'Like Pygmalion?'

'Like Pygmalion,' said Helen, nodding and smiling.

'Then Haxby — Jim — takes them to The Ritz to try out their new skills?' Millie said incredulously

'Yes, that's right. What? Did you think that I'd allow my son to bring young women here merely to seduce them? I promise you, I'm far too old-fashioned for that, Millie.'

'No, of course not,' said Millie, feeling the heat rise to her face. 'I just wondered why I was different. I suppose it's because I'm not as brave and intelligent as the others.'

'That most certainly is not the reason. I wish I could tell you why you're different and why there is no way I'm leaving my son alone with you in your bedroom, but I rather think it's his place to do that.' Her intelligent eyes shone in the firelight. 'And in case you're worrying, it isn't because I disapprove of you. Far from it, child. More people at our agency believed in your father's innocence than you'll ever know. What's more, the loyal daughter who supported his work and who stood by him through his darkest hour is something of a legend amongst us.'

An unbidden tear rolled down Millie's cheek. 'Thank you, Mrs Haxby. You don't know how much that means to me.'

Millie did not know what came over her, but suddenly she was racked with sobs. All the pain she had suppressed over her father's death rose to the fore. Helen Haxby moved from her own chair and put her arms around her, holding her whilst she cried. It felt like being in the arms of the mother who had been missing for most of Millie's life; an emotion that caused both pain and relief.

At one point, Haxby entered the room again and said, 'What is it? What's upset Millie?'

'Her father was unjustly executed,' said Helen quietly, still holding Millie in comforting arms. 'Now go away and leave her with me for a while.'

'But I want to help, Mother.' His hand reached out for Millie's shoulder, but he snapped it back after one sharp look from his mother.

'You can help by letting us girls have this moment alone. Go and talk to Cook about dinner.'

'All right, but I don't like it one bit,' he said, sounding like a petulant ten-year-old. He left the room, slamming the door behind him.

* * *

Over the next few days on Haxby Farm, Millie began to heal, both physically and emotionally. Helen Haxby had a knack of being there when needed and of stepping back when her presence was not required. Millie went out walking, sometimes alone, and sometimes with Helen or Jim — she had finally come to think of him by his diminutive name — accompanying her. Even when alone, she was aware of being watched like a hawk. Not in any sinister way. She sensed they were making sure no one accosted her again, so sometimes she'd see the same gardener several times on her travels, or the same groom, riding one of the horses near the riverbank. Always at a distance, and never intrusive, but always there to ensure her safety.

The best part of being on the farm was that there was no Mrs Oakengate to demand her time. Millie knew that whatever else happened in her life, she would never return to the life of a companion. She considered asking Helen if she could be trained as an agent, but wondered if, even with their kind intentions, her father's alleged crime would go against her.

'I wondered . . . ' she said to Jim one day whilst they were out walking along the river bank, 'whether I'd be a suitable agent.'

'Absolutely not. I forbid it,' he said.

'You forbid it?' Millie stopped and glared at him. The morning sun shone on his dark wavy hair, and he looked more handsome than ever. Which made her feel even angrier about his response. She had wanted him to approve of her, to look up to her as much as she looked up to him.

'It's dangerous work. Do you know what they do to captured agents?'

'I'm aware of it, yes,' said Millie. 'You think I'm not brave enough?'

'I think,' he said, stopping and turning to her, 'that I don't want you to have to cope.'

'Yet you train other young women for the task.'

'They're different.'

'So I'm told,' said Millie archly, walking on. He chased after her, catching her by the arm, spinning her around and pulling her to him.

'Well let's just say they don't run away just because a man has dared to try and make love to them,' he said.

'I'll bet they don't,' said Millie all too aware of his heart beating through the thin fabric of his shirt. If she could feel that, then he must surely feel hers pounding. 'It's a nice little job you've got there, teaching young women about the social . . . niceties.' She knew what she was implying was unjust, and untrue, because of what Helen Haxby had told her, but she was consumed by jealousy over the women whom he obviously thought more capable than her and wondered why he could not see the same intelligence and courage in her.

'That was beneath you, Millie.' He laughed humourlessly, and let go of her arms. 'So perhaps you're not so different to those other girls after all. I'll ask Mother to add you to the waiting list.'

'Don't bother,' she snapped. 'I'll take care of my own employment.'

'And you've done such a good job of taking care of yourself already,' he sneered. 'Almost getting yourself kidnapped by Vasily.'

'How lucky I was that you were there to save me,' she said. 'The intrepid adventurer to the rescue!' She hated herself for the way she behaved, but could not stop the hurtful words tumbling out.

'Next time I'll leave you to the devil.' He turned and walked away, leaving her standing alone by the riverbank.

'Well done, Millie,' she whispered to herself. No wonder he did not think she had the makings of an agent. Her emotions were far too near the surface. She vowed that in future she would behave with much more decorum, especially when alone with Jim Haxby.

She made her way back to the house, and somehow managed to get through the rest of the day. It was clear Helen realised there had been words between

Millie and her son, but she covered it well with interesting conversation. She was a woman for whom silences were anathema, but thankfully not in the same self-absorbed way that Mrs Oakengate did. Helen Haxby simply went out of her way to make everyone in the household happy, be they family, friends or members of staff.

At one point during dinner she looked at Millie and Jim and rolled her eyes in amusement, before moving on to a discussion about how a farmhand's wife was due to give birth within the next few hours. 'I've a feeling there'll be more children around here soon,' she said.

'Why?' said Jim, his face glum and humourless. 'Are all the farmhands' wives with child?'

'Not that I know of,' said Helen, her eyes twinkling. 'But the fresh air here does wonders for that sort of thing. Of course, young people are stupid, and spend far too long skirting around the issue of marriage and children. In fact it seems to be the fashion nowadays to pretend they don't like each other very much. There'd be far more happy events if they just stopped acting so foolishly.'

'I would have thought the happy events were precisely the result of acting foolishly,' said Jim.

'That's because you're a fool, my darling boy,' Helen said mischievously.

'Mother!' Jim looked genuinely hurt. 'I'm not sure what I've done to deserve that.'

'Oh don't take it personally. We're all afflicted with stupidity at times. I have a theory that love affects intelligence. The more in love someone is, the more stupid they become.'

'Really?'

'Yes, really. Now eat your greens. You too, Millie — you'll be needing the iron, child.'

Millie felt as if she had walked in on the middle of a conversation and even then heard only one side of it. She had absolutely no idea what Helen was talking about.

After dinner, she excused herself, saying that she needed an early night. It gave her a chance to be alone with her thoughts.

'Millie,' said Jim, holding the dining room door open for her. His voice was gentler than it had been by the river-bank. 'I'm leaving early in the morning. It's time I tried to track down Chlomsky and get some answers from him. I'll . . . em . . . I'll see you when I return tomorrow night . . . yes?'

She felt like running away again, but had no intentions of doing that. She knew she could not stay at the Haxby's forever, but neither would she disappear in the middle of the night. It would be ungrateful of her, as well as proving to Jim that she was as vapid as he believed.

'Yes, if I'm not imposing by being here,' she said.

'Not at all,' Helen cut in. 'It will be nice to have the company.'

'I'll see you tomorrow night,' said Jim. He reached up and touched her cheek, sending a thrill of delight through her. 'Take care of mother for me.'

'I will,' said Millie, thinking that Helen Haxby was not a woman who needed taking care of. If Jim thought he was paying her a compliment by entrusting his mother's welfare to her, it was too little too late.

'Thank you.' He bent down and placed a tender kiss on her lips, seemingly oblivious to the fact his mother was there.

On her way to her room, Millie vowed that the following day, without Jim there to churn up her emotions, she would talk to Helen about finding employment. Even if she could not be an agent, there might be something she could do in the agency. If that were not possible, she sensed that Helen was a woman with her finger on the pulse and she would know of something Millie could do.

She put on the night clothes that Helen had loaned to her, and got into the big, comfortable bed that she had come to think of as her own. She heard the telephone downstairs ring, and wondered idly who would be calling at this time of the night. Somewhere in the distance a door slammed, and a car started outside. Unable to sleep, she struggled to think of something to do. Just lying there only turned her thoughts to Jim, and he was the last person she wanted to think about. Her mind only kept returning to the kiss outside her hotel room and that way led to sadness and madness. It was then that Millie remembered she still had Barbara Conrad's manuscript. She knew she would have to return it, and felt guilty for not considering it before, but faced with a sleepless night, at around two in the morning, she decided to start reading it, hoping that Barbara would be able to forgive her for running off with it.

As she had found when reading the first few pages, it was very well written and compelling, helping to take her mind off the problems she faced. Before

Millie knew it several hours had passed and, with the coming dawn, she finally started to feel relaxed and sleepy. But the novel had reached a crucial moment, so she read on for a few more pages.

She had reached a point where she began to feel that the paper of the page she was reading felt different. It was not a huge realisation, but a small nagging doubt about the weight. She had got to the bottom of the page, and turned over, only to find that the story seemed to jump forward a few paragraphs. The previous page had ended with the detective's monologue to his sidekick whilst in his office and should have continued over the page. The next page described them as sitting in a restaurant and their discussion had moved on to different matters.

And examination of the next few pages showed the same jumps in time and those pages also felt different and relatively heavy compared to the first pages. Perusing them closely, Millie became aware that several leaves had been stuck together and carried faint water marks. That had happened once to a book she had left out in the rain, and she wondered if that was the problem. Had it been raining when she left The Ritz? She could not remember, but did not think so. But if her bag had somehow got wet, then she was responsible for the damage.

However, attempts to separate the pages met with resistance. They were not waterlogged. They were glued together. Millie held the book open so that she could put one page up to the bedside lamp. There was a darker area in the centre, denoting, Millie suspected, another sheet of paper.

She crept downstairs to the kitchen, where Cook had left the huge copper kettle on the fire stand, no doubt just in case anyone called for a hot drink during the night. It took her a while, but gradually the first glued page began to unstick. It tore slightly at the edges, causing Millie some concern, but eventually she had removed enough glue so that the sheet of paper inside slid out easily.

By the time she finished, there were cight sheets of paper which, when assembled together, made up the facsimile of a blueprint for a massive weapon. She had seen enough of them whilst helping her father with his work to recognise their import.

Put together, they built up the entire picture of the weapon and would no doubt have been very valuable indeed to the agents of another country.

Millie ran upstairs, first to Helen's room, because she was too shy to go to Jim's. There was no answer at the door. So she went on to Jim's, only to find he was not answering either. Not knowing what else to do, Millie went up to the attic rooms and awoke Cook.

'What is it, Miss?' asked Cook, wiping sleep from her eyes.

'Where are the Haxby's?' asked Millie. 'They're not in their rooms.'

'No, Miss. The young master was called away last night on some business.

Mrs Haxby had to leave in the early hours because the farmhand's wife was about to give birth, but there were complications. A breach birth, they say. She should be back soon though it's never sure how long these things will take.'

Millie knew she could not deal with the implications of finding the facsimile on her own, but the two people she knew she could trust were not available. There were so many questions to be answered. The first question involved Barbara Conrad and whether she had known her manuscript was being used to hide secret documents. The more Millie thought about it, the less sense it made. Vasily had been searching the upper rooms of Fazeby Hall, probably for these very documents. If Barbara Conrad were involved in the trade off, she would simply have told Vasily that Millie had them, or just asked Millie for them back. Millie tried to remember what she knew of Barbara Conrad's husband, but it amounted to very little.

Barbara had looked sad when Millie asked about him, but had not offered any information about him. In fact nobody had.

The library in Haxby Farm was a long gallery, filled with ancient volumes and the most recent novels and popular non-fiction. It also included an up to date Who's Who. Millie spent an hour scouring its pages, looking through all the Conrads. None of the men listed was married to a Barbara and Barbara Conrad herself was not listed at all. It did not mean anything — not everyone had a listing in Who's Who. Millie considered how else she might find out.

Jim Haxby had mentioned meeting Mrs Conrad in Argentina. Of course, thought Millie — Alex Markham had been in Argentina for two years. He might know about Mr Conrad. Millie felt a growing sense of comfort that there was one other person she could trust. She went back to the hallway, and despite the early hour put a call through to Fazeby Hall.

'Good morning,' she said to the footman who answered. 'This is Millicent
Woodridge. Is Sir Alexander Markham
still at Fazeby Hall?'

'He is still here, Miss Woodridge.'

'I realise it's very early, but could you
fetch him? It is rather urgent.'

'Certainly, Miss.'

'Millie, my dear girl,' said Alexander
Markham several minutes later. 'We've
been worried sick about you. Where
have you been?'

'Staying with friends,' said Millie, not
wanting to explain any further. 'Uncle
Alex, this may come out of the blue but
what do you know about Barbara
Conrad? Or her husband?'

'Barbara Conrad?' Millie might have
imagined it, but there seemed to be a
slight pause before Alex answered.

'Yes, I remember James Haxby saying
that she was in Argentina, and as you
were there too, I wondered if you'd ever
met her husband, or knew anything
about him.'

'No . . . No, I can't say I have. What

is all this about, Millie?'

'She loaned me her manuscript, and I've found the facsimile of a blueprint stuck into the pages. It's for a weapon, Uncle Alex! I think Count Chlomsky's man, Vasily, was looking for it on Saturday.'

'I see and you think Barbara Conrad is guilty of passing secrets?'

'I'm not sure. You see, she could have just asked me for it back had she known and wanted him to have it. So I don't think she could know.'

'Yes, I see what you mean. So you think her husband is behind it?'

'Well he's a bit mysterious, isn't he? No one seems to know about him, and she doesn't talk about him very much.'

'No, that's true, she doesn't. Look, why don't I find out what I can about Mr Conrad and get back to you? Where are you staying?'

'It's all right,' said Millie. 'I'll come up to you.'

'That's a good idea,' said Alex. 'But don't come to Fazeby Hall. As you can imagine, my dear girl, Mrs Oakengate is not very happy with you at the moment. I'll meet you at the little café at the bottom of Masson Hill. Perhaps then you'll tell me where you've been hiding for the past few days.'

9

Millie scribbled a hasty note, thanking Helen Haxby for her hospitality, and then asked to be taken to the station. At the back of her mind was the nagging doubt that she should let Jim know what she had found, but she still felt angry with him for underestimating her. With Uncle Alex's help, she could solve the mystery of who killed poor Hortense Parker-Trent and her husband, and perhaps find out who was passing secrets to the enemy. It might even lead her to the man or men who had framed her father.

That it might also make Jim admire her was irrelevant — or so she had managed to convince herself by the time she was well on her way back to her uncle in Derbyshire.

The trip from Kent to Derbyshire was a long one, involving a couple of changes. As Millie could not afford First Class, she travelled in Second Class. On the last leg of the journey, she found herself sitting opposite a vacuum cleaner salesman, who had the mistaken idea that everyone in the carriage would be fascinated by his wares.

'I've got a leaflet,' he said, 'if anyone wants one.' According to the leaflets, the vacuum cleaners not only cleaned up dust, but also, apparently improved the class of the average woman. At least judging by the picture of an elegant lady dressed in high fashion, happily vacuuming her staircase.

With little else to do to drown out the salesman, Millie pretended to read Mrs Conrad's manuscript, hoping that he would get fed up of trying to sell to her and turn his attentions on someone else. It was a futile activity, given that so many of the pages were still stuck together, apart from the small openings Millie had made to release the papers. She idly flipped through the pages, then turned to the back page. It was blank, so hardly worth the effort. Millie was just about to turn back to the beginning and start again when she noticed some indentations upon the paper, as if another sheet had been rested upon it whilst someone wrote a note. She held it up the window, before turning to the salesman.

'Excuse me, I don't suppose you have a pencil I might borrow?'

The salesman complied, after which Millie excused herself and went to the restroom, not wanting others to see what she was doing. Holding the manuscript up against the wall, she gently rubbed the pencil across the page. Part of the message was missing, but there was enough to tell Millie all she needed to know . . .

By the time she had reached the café at the bottom of Masson Hill, she had just about managed to compose herself. She had no idea how the meeting would play out, but she knew that whatever happened, she must not climb Masson Hill.

'Millie, there you are,' said Alex

Markham, holding out his hands. The small café was virtually empty, apart from a veiled woman sitting with her back to them. Millie looked at her for a long moment, thinking she might turn around. The woman stared resolutely at the wall in front of her. 'What can I get you? Tea? Coffee?'

'Tea would be nice,' said Millie, flashing her most charming smile, and summoning up her mother's spirit to help her with the part she needed to play. Alex called the waiter and gave their order, after which he helped Millie into her seat.

'You gave us all quite a fright, young lady,' said Alex, taking his own seat. 'Now, do tell all. Where have you been?'

'I went to London, as you know. Then on to the Haxbys' Farm in Kent.'

'The Haxbys? They know you're here, of course.'

'Yes, of course.' Millie only faltered slightly. Helen would most certainly have got her note but Millie had not said where she was going.

'Why did you go there?'

'I was hurt whilst in London. Vasily attacked me.'

'Chlomsky's valet? Oh yes, you mentioned his name this morning.'

'He tried to abduct me, Uncle Alex.' Millie almost choked on the familiar name. 'I think he knew by then that I had the manuscript.'

'Where is it now?'

'Here, in this bag,' said Millie, gesturing to a drawstring bag that she had borrowed from the Haxby's Cook.

'You'd better give it to me,' said Alex. 'I can get it to the right people.'

'The right people or the wrong people, Uncle Alex?' asked Millie.

'I'm not sure what you mean by that,' said Alex. He looked around him. 'That tea seems to be taking an age. Why don't we go for a walk?'

'Up Masson Hill you mean?'

'Yes, why not. Get some fresh air. You look a bit pale.'

Millie put her hand onto the bag. 'How much is this worth to you and your wife, Uncle Alex?'

'I don't have a wife, dear girl. Remember, I asked you to marry me?'

'Yes, you did, didn't you? But it occurs to me that a man who'd send his own friend to the gallows would have no compunction about undertaking a bigamous marriage.'

'That's a rather harsh accusation, dear girl. Who exactly do you think this wife is?' asked Alex, his normally silky voice having become harder and more dangerous.

'I don't think. I know. It's Barbara Conrad. I suppose she uses her maiden name, but just added the Mrs to sound more respectable. So, Uncle Alex, how much is this manuscript worth to you?'

'You're playing a dangerous game, dear girl.' He leaned towards her, and for the first time in her life, Millie became aware of the menace of the man. Funny, thought Millie, how she had never noticed how lizard-like he appeared until that moment. His eyes were narrow slits, and to compound the image, he licked his lips quickly. 'First of all I want to know why you think Barbara Conrad is my wife.'

'There's an imprint of a note on the back of the manuscript.' Millie removed it from the bag, to show him where she had etched over the imprint. The note read, *Promise me that as soon as we've got the money from Vasily, we will go public about our marriage, Alex. With love, Barbara.*

As Millie suspected, Alex snatched the manuscript from her. 'You're a silly girl, Millie. Any fool knows that you don't show the goods until the deal is made. What were you going to ask for? Money? I've already offered you that. Provided you married me.'

'No, a pardon for my father — and you can do that without implicating yourself. I know you can.'

Alex snorted. 'I may be able to, but I don't want to. Getting your father framed for my espionage is one of my greatest achievements. All I had to do was have him photographed with the right people, then plant the relevant documents on him. Richard was so damn trusting, he never saw it coming. In fact, I don't think he ever realised.'

'I wondered why you disappeared for two years,' said Millie, her eyes brimming with tears. 'Guilt, I suppose.'

'Good Lord, no. Guilt is an emotion only felt by fools. I was ensuring no one connected me to your father. Out of sight, out of mind, sort of thing. You really have to learn not to be so sentimental, Millie. That's why you've failed today. There's a part of you that believes good old Uncle Alex will want to do the right thing in the end. Believe me when I say that good old Uncle Alex will do the right thing, but only as it benefits him.' He stood up. 'I'd like to stay and chat, but I must get this to my buyers.'

'There's nothing more I can say to persuade you?' said Millie.

'Nothing.'

'Aren't you worried I'll go the police?'

'You'd have to be alive for that, dear

girl, and I have men surrounding this café. You'll never get out. Oh, it's no good looking for the waiter. He works for me too. The rest of the staff were sent off for the day, due to a gas leak.'

Millie looked to the figure in the corner, but had already guessed who she was. The woman stood up and turned. Her movements were slow, awkward, as though she were in pain. She slowly lifted her veil.

'What?' Alex Markham staggered backwards. Even Millie was surprised. It was not Barbara Conrad as she had thought. The young woman looking at them was Hortense Parker-Trent.

'I heard you,' said Hortense. 'I heard you and Mrs Conrad talking about Millie's father. Then that man — Vasily — pushed me over the cliff.'

'You're dead!' Alex gasped.

'Not quite,' said a familiar voice from the kitchen door. It was Haxby, and he held a gun in his hand. 'Hortense was badly hurt. We only said she was dead to put her killer off his guard. By the way, your man is out back there, nursing a sore head. He seems particularly keen to help us with our enquiries as does your wife, especially after she heard that you asked Millie here to marry you.'

Alex Markham grabbed Millie around the waist and held a gun to her head. 'If you try to interfere, I'll kill her,' he said to Jim. 'Now, get your people out of the way, and let me leave.'

'Let Millie go,' said Jim, pointing his gun at the ground. 'Then we'll talk.'

Alex edged towards the door, dragging Millie with him. 'I'm leaving and taking her with me. When they pay me for these documents, I'll have so much money you'll never find me.' He opened the door. 'Tell them to bring me a car.'

'Take the documents, but leave Millie alone,' said Haxby. 'Then we'll get you the car.' Millie felt Alex Markham shake his head behind her.

'No. You won't shoot me while I'm holding her. Besides, I still have quite a fondness for young Millie here,' he said, grasping her roughly by the arm.

'I despise you,' said Millie, her whole body shaking in fear and revulsion. 'You killed my father.'

'No, my dear, I didn't,' said Alex, pressing Millie closer to him. She felt sick at his touch. 'The government did that for me.' He pulled her outside, where a car stood ready. Several men, including Simon Brady stood around, but kept their weapons facing down.

Markham opened the door, and tried to push Millie into the car. At that point, she kicked against him and managed to break free. She ran back towards the café, hearing shots ring out and fly over her head, then the sound of the car revving up, and driving away.

'I think I got him,' said Jim, catching Millie in his arms. 'Are you alright?'

'Yes, yes, I'm fine. I don't understand, about Hortense . . . how?'

'Calm down, I'll explain to you later. But first we have to get after Markham before he takes those documents away.'

'You really think I was that stupid, don't you?' said Millie, stepping back, angrily. 'To hand them over to him after I found out he was involved.'

'No, of course, I don't think you're stupid, Millie. It was a beginner's mistake, that's all. You were incredibly brave, coming here alone to deal with it. We all think so.'

'Please don't patronise me,' said Millie, glumly. It hurt her to realise that nothing had changed.

'I'm not, darling. All I'm saying is that — '

'Jim,' Brady interrupted, 'we don't have time for all this. We must get that facsimile before it falls into the wrong hands. Come on!'

'That's what I'm trying to tell you,' said Millie, rolling her eyes heavenward. 'Markham doesn't have it.'

'Where is it?' Jim asked.

'At a safe deposit box in the bank. I took it there this morning, before I came to the café.'

'So what does Markham have in the book?'

'Let's just say that I'm sure foreign governments will be fascinated by the possibilities of a new brand of vacuum cleaner,' said Millie.

10

When they assembled at Fazeby hall to share information, Hortense Parker-Trent told them, 'It was Jim's idea.' She looked different than she had on the first day Millie met her. Devoid of make up, Hortense's face looked younger and fresher. There was no doubt she was a very pretty woman and, as the heir to her late husband's fortune, desirable in more ways than one. There was something else different about her. She had lost the frightened air she wore whilst in her husband's company.

They all sat around the dining table. Jim Haxby, Simon Brady, Hortense Parker-Trent, Henry and Cynthia Fazeby, Mrs Oakengate, and Millie, who was doing her best to avoid Mrs Oakengate's furious stares. She knew she would have to face her employer's anger at some point, but the assembled company's interest in the revelations was buying her some time.

'When I fell, Jim — Mr Haxby — climbed down and I told him about the man who pushed me off, though I didn't know the man's name. Jim told me to play dead, so I did. I did tell him to let my husband know the truth,' she added hastily. 'If only I'd known he was going to be in danger,' said Hortense, lapsing into silence. No one said anything, allowing her to compose herself. 'Arthur and I had a complicated relationship, but we loved each other very much. I will miss him dreadfully.'

If Hortense wanted to believe that, then no one in the room would contradict her. It was Millie's belief that Hortense had a lucky escape, but it was fitting that Hortense did not criticise a dead man.

'Where was I?' said Hortense.

'You were telling us about Jim's plot,' said Simon Brady, gently. He looked at Hortense with open admiration.

'Yes, as I said, Jim suggested we pretend I was dead and I think he talked the doctor into saying the same. It seemed a very exciting thing to do,' she said, enthusiastically. 'Like in a book. Em . . . I don't know what happened after that.'

'Hortense was unconscious for several days,' said Jim, picking up the story. 'Not surprising really, considering her fall. So it was a waiting game until she came around and was able to remember more about the man who pushed her off. She also remembered that it was Markham and Barbara Conrad she'd heard talking about Millie's father, Richard Woodridge.'

'Yes,' said Hortense, 'I was in the corridor near to Mrs Conrad's bedroom before you came to see her, Millie. Sir Alexander was with her. She was saying how it was unfair because you're such a nice girl and asking him if there was some way he could undo it. He laughed at her and told her not to be so sentimental.'

'That's why I was called away from Haxby Farm,' Jim said to Millie. 'To get Hortense's statement. Now we can say what we know about Alexander Markham. Any sign of him yet, Brady?'

Simon took a moment to answer, so obviously enchanted was he by Hortense. 'Oh, no, nothing yet. He seems to have disappeared.'

'Alexander Markham was an arch manipulator,' said Jim. 'People trusted him, and he always ensured that there were others to take the blame for him.' Millie swallowed hard. 'Including your father,' said Jim, reaching across and covering her hand with his. 'In Richard Woodridge's case, it was done without his knowledge. Barbara Conrad, however, did the things she did for Markham because she was in love with him.

'She's in custody now, and it was from her we got most of our information, though I don't think everything she said can be taken as gospel. She's obviously trying to save her own neck by putting most of the blame on him.

They met in Argentina, where she went to write her first novel. Markham seduced her then married her, although we have reason to believe that the marriage is not legal. In fact there may be several Markham brides dotted around the globe.' Millie blushed and thanked God she'd had the sense to say no to Markham. 'The blueprint was one that came through Markham's office.'

'He saw the potential immediately,' Jim continued. 'He had no intentions of holding the facsimile himself, so he talked Barbara into hiding it in one of her novels. She was to be the one who did the trade off with Vasily. Now, either because she wanted to hold Markham to ransom, or get more money for both of them out of Vasily, she gave the novel to Millie. She refuses to elaborate on that point. But whatever happened, if the facsimile was found, all suspicion would fall upon Barbara Conrad, and Markham would have no part in it whatsoever. We believe that had Barbara Conrad not found out that Markham proposed to Millie, she would have happily taken the blame for him.' Jim's eyes darkened slightly.

'But what about Chlomsky?' asked Millie. 'What was his part in all this?'

'Chlomsky was, and is, entirely innocent,' said Jim. 'Markham just used him as another scapegoat by planting Vasily as his valet. Believe me when I say that Markham was a man who knew how to cover his tracks. If he couldn't have framed Barbara Conrad, he'd have framed Chlomsky.

'No one in Britain trusts a foreigner, particularly if you place him alongside a pillar of the community, such as Markham. As it is, Chlomsky is a good man, and has even been helping us piece together the facts about Vasily and discovered that he was actually an intermediary for a foreign government intent on getting their hands on the weapon blueprints.'

'What went wrong this time?' asked Simon Brady. 'Why did Markham get so careless?'

'He was getting desperate for the

manuscript,' said Jim. 'According to Barbara Conrad the buyers were threatening to pull out and Markham was running short of money. So when Millie told him she had it, he believed she would hand it over quite readily, trusting him to do the right thing. I must say he was surprisingly careless.'

'That's because he underestimated me,' said Millie. 'Many people do.'

'I'm sure that's not true, dear girl,' said Henry Fazeby, kindly.

'The important thing, Millie,' said Jim, sounding impatient, 'is that your father is innocent. Barbara Conrad has given us the evidence we need to prove that. Believe it or not, despite everything, I think she actually likes you. She said that one of the best things about it being all over was that you'd know for sure your father was innocent.'

'I've always known that,' said Millie, her voice catching in her throat. 'Only it's too late now, isn't it?' She wanted to leave the room but it came to her with a startling and painful realisation that she had nowhere to go.

She was no longer a staying guest at the Fazeby's, so could not run to the room they had given her the first time and she had no other home to which she could run. If only she could think straight, she would know what to do. But the revelations had shaken her to the core. How could the man whom her father had called his best friend have sent him to the gallows? Millie had trusted him too, until the truth of the note on the back of the manuscript had taught her otherwise. How could she ever trust her instincts about people again?

'Well, of course, I've always known dear Richard was innocent,' said Mrs Oakengate. 'And given the events, Millie, I am quite willing to forgive you for your gallivanting and take you back as my companion.'

'I'm very grateful, Mrs Oakengate,' said Millie, 'but I have decided that I'm not cut out to be a paid companion. Well, at least, I'm not cut out to be your paid companion.'

'Really,' said Mrs Oakengate. 'Well, what do you think of that, Cynthia? I give the girl my charity and this is how she repays me.'

'Perhaps Millie would prefer friendship and equality to charity,' said Cynthia Fazeby.

'Millie,' said Hortense, sounding shy, 'I'm going to be running Arthur's businesses from now on. That probably means a lot of old men in suits will bully me. Is it possible, if you've got nothing else planned, that you could work for me as a personal assistant? You're much braver than I am. Don't worry about not knowing anything about the business. Neither do I, but we could learn together.'

Millie looked up in amazement. 'Yes, yes, of course. That would be wonderful. Thank you. But you really mustn't put yourself down, Hortense. It took a lot of courage to do what you did.'

'Hear hear,' said Simon Brady.

'Hear hear,' said Jim Haxby, with rather less enthusiasm.

11

Millie turned from her contemplation of the Fazeby Hall gardens. It was getting dark and drizzling with rain outside, but her bedroom was warm and cosy. When she had made to leave the house — to go she knew not where — Cynthia Fazeby had insisted she stay as a guest in her own right. As soon as she could do so without being ill-mannered, she went to her room to escape Mrs Oakengate's fury. Odd, she thought to herself that she could stand up to her godfather, yet facing Mrs Oakengate still filled her with abject terror. She had to remind herself who was the most deadly of the two, but in truth, she was not so sure.

'Millie?' an all-too-familiar voice said.

'What is it, Mr Haxby?'

Jim paused a moment, and she sensed her sudden return to formality had perplexed him. It felt safer for her to think of him in formal terms, protecting her heart from further pain. 'I just wanted to say what a wonderful thing you did today. It was very resourceful of you. I'd never have thought of that.'

She searched his face for signs that he was patronising her, but he seemed to be speaking honestly. 'If you knew the conversation I had to endure with the vacuum cleaner salesman just to get his brochures, you'd be saying I deserved a medal.' She smiled mischievously. 'I know more about their inner workings than I ever wanted to.'

'Believe me, I've met a few salesmen on my travels. I'll write to the king and demand you get a Victoria Cross.' He smiled and the icy barrier she had put around her heart melted. They were right back where they began, with no awkwardness between them. It lifted an immense weight from her shoulders. 'Look, Millie, all the things I said about you not being an agent. You know, forbidding you and all that . . . '

Millie held up her hand and shook her head. 'It really doesn't matter. I was just being silly.'

'I don't think it's at all silly to want to help your country.'

'No, what I meant was . . . well, it was all tied up in wanting to impress you. Because you're . . . well you're the adventurer, James Haxby. A man one wants to impress. I behaved like a schoolgirl meeting a matinee idol. Then London happened and my emotions got the better of me . . . I know you'll think me foolish. I mean, all those women you work with, they're so self-assured and . . . '

She did not have to say any more. He pulled her into his arms and kissed her. 'You must know how I feel about you,' he said when he reluctantly stopped. 'You don't have to try to impress me. You've impressed me right from the very beginning, my darling Grey Lady. When Markham had that gun to your head . . . ' He took a deep breath, as if the pain of the memory were too much for him. 'I never want to see you in that danger again, my darling. And I'm sorry if I gave you the impression I thought you incapable. I knew you were brave the moment I saw you at the top of the stairs. But I didn't want you to have to be brave. You looked so vulnerable, with those big sad eyes, and I had this immediate need to protect you and keep you from harm. You realise, don't you, that no other woman on Earth has made me behave like such a caveman.'

'Caveman or not, I love you,' she whispered against his chest, her whole body tingling from his touch and the wonderful things he was saying to her. He kissed her head, her face, her nose, her lips.

'It would scandalise everyone if I stayed in your room any longer,' he murmured against her throat. He traced kisses around her neck, sending a million tiny electric shocks down her spine.

'It would devastate me if you left.'

They lay on the bed together, talking and kissing far into the night. He promised her that he would go to London the next day to set in motion the clearing of her father's name. It made her cry again but he gently wiped the tears away. 'One day, I swear you'll be happy again,' he vowed.

'Believe it or not, I'm happy now,' she said before another tear rolled down her cheek. His lips caught it before it fell to the pillow.

★　★　★

When she woke in the morning, he had left her side. Although she suspected he had left early to spare her reputation, nevertheless she still felt the ache of his absence. She assured herself he would return. He had promised, had he not?

Despite her lack of sleep, Millie agreed to go with Hortense and Simon Brady on a trip to The Heights of Abraham, in the hopes that the fresh air would revive her. Well, that and the fact that Mrs Oakengate cast dark looks at her all through breakfast, muttering something about 'needing to have a good talk to some people'.

'Victoria, my dear,' said Henry Fazeby from behind his paper. 'There's a young girl here in need of your patronage. Her father has just been convicted of murdering her mother.'

'Spousal murder is such a common crime,' said Mrs Oakengate.

'The murderer is the youngest son of a duke.'

'Really? Of course, murder among the upper classes is a much more civilised affair. You must give me the details, Henry. I'm sure she can't turn out worse than my last companion.'

'Cynthia and I rather like her,' said Henry with a mischievous wink. 'Almost part of the family, in fact.'

Millie smiled at him, silently blessing him for his kindness.

★　★　★

'I need to face that cliff,' said Hortense, as they put on their coats. 'I still have nightmares about it, and I'm hoping that going there will stop them.'

'It's early days,' said Simon. 'You mustn't force yourself.'

'Simon is right, Hortense,' said Millie. 'We don't have to go there.'

'I do.' Hortense reached out her hand and took Millie's. 'That hill belongs to me, not the person who pushed me off. I intend to go up there and reclaim it.'

'She's wonderful, isn't she?' said Simon.

'Yes, she is,' said Millie, understanding why no one had noticed it before. The shadow of Arthur Parker-Trent had lifted, leaving his young wife standing in the sunlight.

Rather than walk, because Hortense still suffered the after-effects of her plummet over the cliffs, they took the cable car. She looked apprehensive, but remained calm when they reached the Heights and looked out over the view. On such a glorious spring morning it was hard to believe that anything bad could happen to anyone. Hortense was young, beautiful, with the world at her feet and a man who was clearly beginning to adore her. There were few other people around, meaning that the three friends practically had the Heights to themselves.

'I wonder if they'll ever find Markham,' said Hortense. Millie shivered, and it was as if a cloud passed over the sun.

'I don't think so,' Simon said. 'He'll have found a way to get out of the country by now.'

'He's a wicked man,' Hortense said. It seemed to help her to talk about it. She had been so resilient that it had not even occurred to Millie that she might have been affected psychologically. Hortense was the sort of person who got on with things, but such people usually hid their fears deep down.

'They make them like that in Derbyshire,' said Simon, when Millie said as much to him. 'Though she's not the only survivor around here.'

'I don't know that I'm as ready to face my demons,' said Millie, and once again she shivered.

There was something in the air, something close. She wished Jim were with them. Not that she could not trust Simon to protect them, but it was simply not the same.

When Hortense and Simon suggested walking back down to the café, Millie excused herself, saying that she wanted to stay a while longer. She smiled at them as they walked down the hill together, taking their first tentative steps towards what Millie hoped would be a lasting love affair. It was early days for Hortense, but there was no reason why she should not find happiness with Simon.

'Be careful, dearest,' Hortense called back.

Millie waved back then turned and looked out over Derbyshire. She could see why Hortense loved it so.

So much had happened and here she was, right back where it all started only a few days earlier. It seemed like centuries ago. She remembered that first morning, going down the hill with Haxby, and her secret thrill at being his walking partner. She remembered the way he defended her father in the café. How handsome he looked at the Ritz, and the kiss that came afterwards. At his mother's house, he had treated her with immense tenderness, even though she had made him angry. She even managed to laugh when she remembered him saying, 'I forbid it' after she asked about being an agent. Would their time together be a constant battle of wills? Perhaps, but it most certainly would not be dull.

No man had ever seemed so alive to her, or made her feel so alive. She hoped she was enough for him. His kisses of the night before seemed to say that she was. He had once said he was not a nice man, but she believed that was a lie he told himself in order to accomplish the difficult work he had to do. He was more than just a nice man;

he was a good man. One who was not afraid to fight for what he believed was right. She smiled at the notion that the redoubtable Helen Haxby would allow her son to be anything other.

Whatever else happened, whether they stayed together or not, Millie would never regret the moments she spent in Haxby's arms.

Behind her, footsteps cracked on ground roots. Millie spun around, half hoping it would be Jim. It was not. At first she barely recognised the man who approached her. His clothes were grimy and covered in twigs, as if he had been sleeping in a box all night, his face dirty and unshaven.

'Surprised to see me, Millie?' he asked.

'Uncle Alex!' The familiar term came unbidden, for he had ceased to be the fond godfather of her childhood.

'I've waited for this moment,' he said. 'There was no chance of getting to you at Fazeby Hall with your champion in attendance. He soon left didn't he? You should learn, child, that a man won't buy the cow if he can have the milk for free.'

Millie wanted to argue but it seemed irrelevant under the circumstances. A man like Markham would never understand such a thing as trust anyway. He lived a life of lies and betrayal and assumed everyone else behaved in the same way. The simple values of the real world were beyond his ken. She almost pitied him for it, but steeled herself against him by remembering what he had done to her father. And she did trust Jim, despite the foolish doubts that she knew only came from loving him so deeply and only just starting to believe he felt the same. She remembered his kisses to fortify herself. 'You've been watching me.'

'Oh, yes.' He reached forward, his hands outstretched like claws. 'Like I said, I've waited for this moment. As if I, Alexander Markham could be fooled by a stupid little girl.'

'Except I'm not stupid,' said Millie.

'You got lucky,' he said. 'If you hadn't found the inscription of her note you'd never have known. It's a pity Millie. You could have been my wife.'

'Another for your harem?' Millie laughed humourlessly. Once the initial shock of seeing Alex Markham had abated, Millie began to realise the seriousness of her position. She had her back to the cliff, and he was slowly moving towards her. Only a few feet separated them. She looked around quickly, to see if there were any other walkers, but the only ones nearby were on the hill, too far away to be of any help to her. She thought of screaming, just to get someone's attention, but she feared that might simply make the situation worse.

'You'd have been the only one, Millie.'

'Perhaps,' said Millie, thinking on her feet, 'I still could be. No one has seen you. We could go away from here.'

'And the minute you got amongst people, you'd scream at the top of your lungs. You fooled me once, Millie. That won't happen again. Do you know how much planning it took to achieve the things I did?'

'I think I have an idea how many others paid for your plans.'

'I'm sorry about your father. Truly I am. Richard was my best friend, but they were closing in on me and I had to think quickly. He was the only other person who had been in the same places as me.'

'What about Barbara Conrad? She might be executed too. Don't you feel the least bit sorry about her?'

'She was a damn fool, taking to you the way she did. I should have known better than to trust a woman.'

'She loved you and now she's going to die for that.'

'I know, I made sure of that. If I'd had more time with you . . . '

A faint breeze stirred some nearby bushes, catching Alex's attention. Millie took the opportunity to run in the opposite direction, along the cliff edge, before trying to make her way down. She was not quick enough. Alex, despite his age and condition, managed to head her off, catching her arms in a vice-like grip.

'Not so quick,' he said, pulling her back up the hill after him, and back along towards the cliff edge. 'You will pay for what you've done to me.'

'I've done nothing to you,' said Millie, pulling frantically in the opposite direction. 'You're the one who's ruined your life, by betraying your friends and your loved ones.'

'I'd have succeeded, too, if not for you.' He twisted her wrist, making her cry out in pain. Despite wanting to remain calm, Millie felt tears sting her eyes. She had her body turned away from Markham, still trying to get back down the hill. If she let him, he would push her over the cliff and she did not want to take the chance that there would be a handy ledge to break her fall. For his part, Markham had his full attention on Millie. It was a battle of wills that cut out everything else around them, like they were the only two people left in the world.

'No, you'd have failed eventually, with or without my help. Men like you do, because they betray so many people, they find themselves with no friends, no one to turn to.'

'Who have you got now, Millie, eh? Your father is dead, Your stupid friend is too busy with her new love, and Haxby has no doubt gone off to find someone more interesting than some pale-faced little idiot who sits up and begs the moment he asks her to.'

'Far from it,' a familiar voice said. Millie looked up through her tears, and saw Jim standing to the left of Markham, a gun pointed at the older man's temple. He was also dishevelled, but in a rather more attractive way, his hair tousled on his head. He wore a pair of jodhpurs and a white shirt, open at the neck. 'I must say tracking you down hasn't been that interesting. Only necessary. I knew you'd come after

Millie eventually.'

Markham spun around, almost managing to knock the gun out of Jim's hand. There was a struggle, as each man tried to gain superiority over the other. As they fought, they moved nearer to the cliff edge.

'Jim, darling, no!' screamed Millie, as Markham almost succeeded in pushing him over. But Jim regained his footing and the upper hand. Instead of trying to push Markham over the cliff, Jim clearly sought to contain him, but Markham was determined not to be taken.

How long they fought was hard to say. To Millie it all seemed to happen slowly, only speeding up when the fight reached its most dangerous, near to the edge of the cliff.

She wanted to help, to stop Jim being hurt, so a few times she rushed forward, to try and drag Markham off. He, in turn, swatted her as if she were a fly, throwing her to the ground, and almost sending her over the cliff. Jim grabbed for her skirt, then her arms, pulling her back from the precipice and, in doing so, lost the gun over the edge. When Millie saw Markham about to rush Jim whilst his attention was taken in helping her, she was able to stick her foot out. Markham lurched forward, and hurtled over the edge of the cliff.

There were no ledges to save Markham. They saw him plummet right down to the bottom and heard his piercing cry. Millie hid her head in Jim's shoulder, the horrific sound sending a shudder throughout her body.

'It's all right, darling, you're safe now,' Jim said gently, pulling her into his arms and kissing her passionately.

12

Despite her protests to the contrary, Millie was made to go to bed early. 'I'm perfectly all right,' she told Helen Haxby, who had arrived hotfoot from Kent whilst they were out.

'My dear girl,' said Helen, after they told her everything that had happened, 'You've had two very stressful days. These things have a habit of catching up with you. Now go and get some rest, and if you're very good, I might let Jim come up and see you.'

Jim's kiss still burned her lips. He had held her all the way back to Fazeby Hall and almost had to be peeled off her by his mother, whilst the others excitedly asked what had happened.

So she lay in her darkened room, frustrated beyond belief. She wanted to know why Jim had not told her he was going after Markham.

It was getting late when she heard a knock at the door, and Jim entered, carrying a tray. 'I'm allowed to bring you a hot drink, but I have to leave straight away.'

'I wish you wouldn't,' said Millie.

'In that case,' he said, smiling, 'I'll stay a while and risk the wrath of your two mothers, Helen and Cynthia, waiting downstairs. Not to mention Henry, who has all but challenged me to a duel if I dare to bring your good name into disrepute. Have you any idea just how many people love you?' He sat on the edge of the bed, but annoyingly put the tray carrying the drink between them. 'How are you feeling, my love?'

'I'm feeling perfectly fine,' said Millie. 'Despite what people think, I'm not some helpless woman who needs to lie down for three days after every dramatic incident.'

'No one thinks that, darling, though I did have to save your life today.'

'I rather thought it was I who saved your life.' Millie's eyes twinkled.

'Yes you did, which of course means I am now beholden to you for the rest of my life.'

'I don't know that I want you to be beholden to me, James Haxby.'

'Oh, but I am, my love. You've saved me from a life of utter selfishness. I never wanted to get married, but with you it's all I can think about.' He pulled her into his arms, sweeping away the tray. Millie's heart flipped. Despite her silent affirmations, what Markham had said had played on her own doubts. She lay her head against Jim's chest, hearing his heart beat in time with hers. 'When I saw Markham grab you near the edge of the cliff. Dear God, I thought I was too late.' He kissed her for a long time.

'I love you,' said Millie, when he set her lips free again.

'I heard what Markham said to you, and he was wrong.' Jim brushed a stray lock of Millie's hair from her face. 'And another thing, whilst you're determined to think I'm some kind of cad, I didn't take you to London to seduce you either. I had to get you away from that awful Mrs Oakengate somehow. She was determined to keep us apart, and I had no intentions of letting that happen.'

'I think she's a terribly lonely woman,' said Millie, whose joy was making her feel charitable towards even Mrs Oakengate. 'Why didn't you tell me you were tracking Markham today?'

'Because I didn't want to worry you about him still being in the area. It's the caveman in me wanting to protect you again. Can you allow me that?'

Millie tilted her face upwards and kissed his chin. 'I find it quite impossible to refuse you anything.'

'Careful, I might want to prove that theory and Henry is a much better shot than me. We'll go to London together to clear your father's name, darling, because it's something you really should be there for. But for now let's forget all the awful things that have happened and discuss wonderful things like marriage and babies.' They were just about to kiss again when . . .

'Jim,' said a voice from the door. 'I rather think the babies can wait until after the wedding, don't you?'

'Mother, we're in love!'

'Wonderful, I'll let everyone know you're engaged. They'll be sure to want to come and congratulate you. Now make sure Millie looks presentable. You've ruffled all her hair up.' Helen swept from the room, smiling broadly.

'Mothers,' muttered Jim.

Millie stroked either side of his handsome face and kissed him, happy to risk further ruffling until the others arrived.

THE END

We do hope that you have enjoyed reading this large print book.

Did you know that all of our titles are available for purchase?

We publish a wide range of high quality large print books including:
Romances, Mysteries, Classics
General Fiction
Non Fiction and Westerns

Special interest titles available in large print are:
The Little Oxford Dictionary
Music Book, Song Book
Hymn Book, Service Book

Also available from us courtesy of Oxford University Press:
Young Readers' Dictionary
(large print edition)
Young Readers' Thesaurus
(large print edition)

For further information or a free brochure, please contact us at:
Ulverscroft Large Print Books Ltd.,
The Green, Bradgate Road, Anstey,
Leicester, LE7 7FU, England.
Tel: (00 44) **0116 236 4325**
Fax: (00 44) **0116 234 0205**

WILD FOR LOVE

Carol MacLean

Polly is an ecologist, passionate and uncompromising about wildlife rights. Against all her principles she falls in love with Jake, heir to a London media empire, whose development company is about to destroy a beautiful marsh. But can love ever blossom between two such different people? As Polly battles to save the marsh and learns to compromise for love, Jake finally finds the life he has always desired . . .

FREE FALL

Phyllis Humphrey

Jennifer Gray, working with Colin Thomas on a sports promotion, doesn't like her job. He's a pilot, skydiver and owner of Skyway Aviation — and she's afraid of heights! Despite feelings of jealousy over Colin's love interest, he's not the man for her. However, Colin, knows a good thing when he sees it. So will his humour, sensitivity and old-fashioned charm help Jennifer overcome her fear of heights and convince her their relationship is just what she needs?